FROM THE
NANCY DREW FILES

THE CASE: New accusations from an old trial charge Nancy's father with doing something illegal.

CONTACT: A mysterious message draws Nancy into a deadly web of lies and larceny.

SUSPECTS: Kate and Chris Gleason—*the grieving heirs to a bitter trial share a grudge against Nancy's father.*

Cheryl Pomeroy—*the pretty bookkeeper may be merging romance and robbery.*

Edward Vaughn—*the lawyer is bringing charges against Carson Drew on behalf of a dead man.*

COMPLICATIONS: Nancy's father wants her off the case—*any evidence she finds could be used against him.*

Books in The Nancy Drew Files® Series

Available from ARCHWAY Paperbacks

THE NANCY DREW FILES™ CASE • 40

SHADOW OF A DOUBT

Carolyn Keene

AN ARCHWAY PAPERBACK
Published by POCKET BOOKS
New York   London   Toronto   Sydney   Tokyo   Singapore

This book is a work of fiction. Names, characters, places and incidents are either the product of the author's imagination or are used fictitiously. Any resemblance to actual events or locales or persons, living or dead, is entirely coincidental.

AN ARCHWAY PAPERBACK *Original*

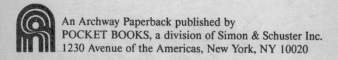

An Archway Paperback published by
POCKET BOOKS, a division of Simon & Schuster Inc.
1230 Avenue of the Americas, New York, NY 10020

Copyright © 1989 by Simon & Schuster Inc.
Cover art copyright © 1989 Jim Mathewuse
Produced by Mega-Books of New York, Inc.

ISBN: 0-671-67492-7

First Archway Paperback printing October 1989

10 9 8 7 6 5 4 3 2

Printed in the U.S.A.

IL 7+

Chapter

One

Nancy Drew heard a click and then the long buzz of a dial tone.

"Who was that, Nan?" her friend George Fayne asked, curious.

The girls were in Nancy's bedroom, getting ready to go out to dinner with Nancy's father, Carson Drew. George's cousin, Bess Marvin, was putting a last coat of Marvelous Red polish on her fingernails.

"Who did you say it was?" Bess asked without looking up.

Nancy shrugged and put the phone back on the hook. "Wrong number, I guess. Whoever it was hung up, anyway."

"Well, if it was Ned, he'll call back. He wouldn't hang up on purpose," Bess said comfortingly.

Ned Nickerson was Nancy's steady boyfriend, but she didn't get many chances to see him because he was away at school, at Emerson College.

Hearing Ned's name made Nancy think about his warm brown eyes and good looks. A slow smile spread across her face as she imagined herself in his arms. Then a long sigh from Bess brought Nancy back to earth.

"Whatever you wear looks great on you," Bess said to her. Nancy was wearing a hip-length slate blue cashmere sweater over black satin pants.

"Bess, you're terrific for my ego," Nancy replied, smiling and pushing her reddish blond hair back from her face. One quick glance in the mirror told her that the sweater had been a good choice. It complemented the graceful curves of her slim figure and brought out the blue in her eyes.

"Why on earth did I buy this dress?" Bess asked, slipping in front of Nancy to look at herself in the mirror. She smoothed the soft, gray jersey over her hips. "It doesn't do a thing for me. If only I had lost five pounds before tonight."

Nancy grinned. With her long blond curls and bright blue eyes, Bess was a knockout.

"You look gorgeous. And anyway, it's only dinner with my father," she told her friend.

"Sure. But you never know when you're going to meet a cute waiter," Bess said.

Bess's cousin, George Fayne, shook her head and rolled her eyes at Nancy. "In her case it's probably true. She will meet an adorable waiter," she said. George leaned into Nancy's vanity mirror and fluffed out her short brown hair.

"Okay, okay." Nancy intervened. "Are you two ready? Our reservation's for eight o'clock. If we don't leave now, we'll be late."

Nancy pushed Bess and George out of her bedroom and down the stairs into the living room.

"Hannah!" Nancy exclaimed. The Drews' housekeeper, Hannah Gruen, had put on a red silk dress and a dash of lipstick.

"It's not often that I get to have dinner with a handsome man at River Heights's best French restaurant," Hannah said, smiling at the surprised looks on Nancy, Bess, and George's faces.

Nancy was about to tell Hannah how nice she looked when the phone rang. She stepped across the living room to answer it. "Hello?"

Instead of a response, Nancy again heard the click of someone hanging up and then a dial tone. She slowly replaced the phone.

"No one there?" George asked.

Nancy shook her head. "It's probably nothing." She paused. "I just wonder——"

"Wonder what, Nan?" Bess asked.

Hannah Gruen looked questioningly at Bess and then at Nancy.

"It's nothing, Hannah," Nancy confidently told her. "It's just a crank call."

Hannah shrugged. "If you say so, Nancy. But maybe you'd better mention it to your father."

"It's nothing to worry about, Hannah," Bess said. "It happens all the time. About a month ago my mom was getting them, but in the end——"

"Why don't you tell us in the car on the way to the restaurant?" George interrupted. "I'd hate to keep Mr. Drew waiting."

Nancy smiled. George was better than anyone at distracting Bess and keeping her chatter to a minimum.

The three friends and Hannah piled into Nancy's Mustang for the short drive across town to Chez Louis.

As she swung around the circular drive that fronted the cozy, cottage-style French restaurant, Nancy smiled to herself. Only her dad would think to treat all of them to dinner at one of the best restaurants in River Heights, she thought. She had been there several times before with Ned, holding hands while watching the sun set over the river.

"Hey, Nancy, wake up." Bess was outside the car, standing beside the driver's window. "There's a valet here who's dying to park your Mustang. And I'm starving."

Nancy laughed and stepped out of her car. "I'm glad to hear it, Bess, because the food at Chez Louis is better than great," she said, following Bess, George, and Hannah inside. There, the maître d', Antoine, was waiting.

"Bonsoir, ladies, good evening," Antoine said, greeting them.

"Bonsoir, Antoine," Nancy answered.

He led them across the restaurant to a table where her father was waiting. Carson Drew was River Heights's most distinguished lawyer. Nancy was proud of her tall, handsome father.

"Are these the four lovely women you were expecting?" Antoine asked with a twinkle in his eye.

"And right on time." Carson stood up and gave Nancy a kiss on the forehead. He smiled at Bess and George, then turned to Hannah. "You look terrific!"

Hannah blushed as Antoine held out her chair. "Thank you," she said, sitting down and unfolding her napkin.

Nancy, Bess, and George took their seats around the circular table as Antoine handed them their menus.

"I hope you're all in the mood for a good

dinner," Carson said, "because this is the place for it."

While they were reading their menus, deciding what to order, Nancy took in the restaurant's plush surroundings. A pleasant glow of candlelight made the elegant silverware set on starched white tablecloths shine. At the far end of the restaurant, where huge windows overlooked the river, couples carried on hushed conversations over their meals.

With a smile Nancy returned her attention to the menu. "Well, I think I know what I want," she said finally. "How about you, Bess?"

Bess gave Nancy a confused look. "I'm not sure yet. There's so much to choose from!"

"You said it," George replied. "And it all looks good. Look, they've even got frogs' legs!"

Carson laughed. "I know they sound strange, but actually they're quite delicious."

Nancy half listened as her father told them about a trip to Paris he'd taken a few years earlier and the frogs' legs he'd eaten there. Nancy's thoughts wandered. She was trying to make some sense of the timing or frequency of the phone calls she'd been receiving. It was no use, though. She had drawn a blank.

"Is everything okay, Nancy?" her father asked.

"I can tell you're still thinking about those phone calls, aren't you?" Hannah said pointedly.

George and Bess exchanged a look. "Let's order," George said. The waiter was standing beside their table now, smiling at them.

"I'll have the artichoke appetizer and the cassoulet," Nancy told him.

"Mussels and steak tartare for me," George put in.

Bess fumbled. "Um, vichyssoise and—an omelet."

"Good choice, Bess," Carson said with a smile. He ordered for both Hannah and himself. "We'll have the Caesar salad and steak au poivre, medium rare. How does that sound?"

"Wonderful," Hannah said. "I just couldn't decide."

The waiter left. Carson turned to Nancy. "Now, what's this about phone calls?" he asked.

"I didn't want to bother you, but we've been getting phone calls lately where the caller hangs up as soon as I answer. I got two more tonight just before we left the house."

"Actually I did take a couple myself, but I didn't realize there were a lot of them," Carson said with a frown.

George looked at her friend. "The solution is simple, Nan—go to the police tomorrow and ask them to trace the calls. Then they can stop whoever's behind them."

"That's a wonderful idea, George," Hannah said.

"You're right, Hannah," Nancy said, brightening. "I'll call Chief McGinnis first thing."

"I'm glad that's solved," Carson said, as the waiter brought over their appetizers. "I'm just as concerned as you are, Nancy, but I was looking forward to a night without mystery." He winked at Bess and George.

Nancy laughed. "You're right, Dad. Now, why isn't everybody eating?"

"I don't think I'll be able to eat for days," Bess groaned as she dropped onto the sofa in the Drews' living room.

"I'm not surprised. You polished off everything, including dessert," George teased.

"I know. But I'm not going to feel guilty. You only live once, after all."

Hannah laughed. "You tell her, Bess."

"I think Antoine has a crush on you, Hannah," Carson said with a smile. "He doesn't kiss everyone's hand, you know."

"Those French men are incredible," George said, giggling. "Romance must be their middle name!"

"I can't wait to go back to Paris—" Bess began. The doorbell rang, interrupting her.

"I'll get it," Hannah said, walking to the front door. "It's awfully late for anyone to come to visit."

"A package for Carson Drew," a young, blond-haired guy said after Hannah had opened the door.

She looked quizzically at the young man. "Thanks," she finally said, and took the envelope.

"This is strange—a young man just brought this for you," she said, handing the large manila envelope to Carson.

Carson took it from her. "That is strange," he said. "Who would send me something so late at night?"

After he opened the envelope and took out the contents, Nancy watched as a confused look passed over her father's face.

"What is it?" she asked.

"I'm not sure." Carson showed the photograph that had been inside to Nancy.

It was a shot of a well-dressed man, sitting behind a desk. The skyline of River Heights appeared in a window behind him.

Nancy looked up at her father, puzzled. "What's this all about?" she asked.

"Probably some crank," he answered slowly.

Nancy took the photograph in her hands to study it more closely. With a shock, she noticed that someone had written in small block letters across the bottom of the picture.

"You can't pretend anymore, Carson Drew. Soon everyone in River Heights will know you hid the evidence that proved this man's guilt!"

Chapter

Two

QUESTIONS TUMBLED through Nancy's head. Why would anyone accuse her father of such a thing? Who was the man in the photograph? Did her father know him? Judging from the look on her father's face, Nancy could tell he was taking the threat seriously.

"What does all this mean?" she asked finally, her voice calm and businesslike.

Before her father could answer, Bess, George, and Hannah had joined them, and they were looking at the photograph now.

"This is crazy," Bess blurted out. "Who would accuse you of hiding evidence?" she asked.

"Who is this guy, anyway?" George asked.

"Hold on, everyone," Carson said, raising a hand. "One at a time, please."

Carson sighed, then took another look at the photograph. "That man is Dennis Allard, and now he's employed as a banker at River Heights Bank and Trust. Eight years ago he was accused of embezzlement. I defended him and he was found innocent."

"Whoever sent this photograph doesn't think he was innocent," Nancy pointed out.

Carson had turned and was staring out the large window that faced the street. After a minute he continued to speak.

"This sort of thing happens all the time," he said. "But usually it's judges who get harassed. I can't remember the last time I heard of a lawyer having this kind of problem . . ." His voice trailed off as he stood there, his back to the room, his eyes fixed and staring.

Nancy knew there was more to this threat than her father was letting on. Someone was making a serious accusation against him, and she would have to find out who and why.

"Why don't you tell us about the case?" she asked gently, leading him back to the sofa. "Maybe with the five of us, we can come up with some idea of who's behind this."

Hannah came back into the living room, carrying a fresh pot of tea and sodas for the girls. "It looks like it's going to be a long night," she explained.

"Thanks, Hannah," Carson said, and indicated that everyone should sit. He cleared his throat and began. "Eight years ago Dennis Allard was accused of embezzling a huge amount of money from the clients of a large law firm here in River Heights."

"But he was innocent," George said.

"As far as I was concerned, he was," Carson told her.

"How was he supposedly embezzling?" Nancy asked. She had to have all the details.

"It was pretty uncomplicated, actually, Nancy." Carson paused. "The law firm where Allard worked, Mobley and Myerson, got complaints from some very important clients that they were being overcharged. When the firm investigated, they found out that someone in the accounting department had been sending out phony bills."

"The firm didn't know that had been going on? How could that happen?" Nancy asked.

"Good question." Carson poured himself a mug of tea, stood up, and began pacing the living room. He held the mug in two hands. "That was exactly what I asked: How could anyone embezzle from the clients of a law firm without the firm knowing what was going on?"

"It must have taken a lot of nerve to do

13

that," Bess said. "To try to embezzle under the noses of a group of lawyers would be impossible."

Carson sat down and loosened his tie. He continued. "Dennis Allard worked in the firm's accounting department. His assistant was a man named Robert Gleason. When the firm discovered that their clients were being overbilled, they knew the embezzlers had to be in the accounting department."

"Dennis Allard," Nancy said, simply.

"Allard, yes—and Gleason, too," Carson said. "The firm prosecuted both Allard and Gleason. I defended Allard, and an attorney named Edward Vaughn defended Gleason. Allard was acquitted, but Gleason was found guilty."

"Someone is obviously still bitter about it," Hannah said. "But everyone deserves a fair trial, and that's what you did for this man." She pointed at the photograph that was lying on the coffee table. "That's what's important."

"Thank you, Hannah," Carson said, smiling. "But someone seems to think I did something illegal."

"And we're going to find out who it is," Nancy said firmly. She tried to get them back on track. "What kind of evidence turned up at Allard's trial?" she asked.

"Nothing substantial," Carson answered. "That's why he was acquitted. In fact, as the evidence was shown, I became more and more convinced that Allard had to be innocent. There wasn't anything concrete to make me think he was guilty."

"But that wasn't true about Gleason? I mean, all the evidence must have pointed to him, right?" Nancy concluded.

Carson smiled at his daughter. "Absolutely," he said.

"Why?" Nancy asked.

George was leaning forward in her chair now. From the looks on their faces, Nancy knew that George and Bess felt a case brewing.

"The prosecution found a document on the firm's computer system. Obviously Gleason assumed no one would find it. The file showed how money was taken in from the firm's clients."

"But how can that one file prove *who* did it?" Bess asked.

"Good point. It can't. Except that only Gleason had access to that program," Carson said. "Therefore he had to be involved."

Nancy bit on her lower lip, thinking. "What exactly was in that program, Dad?" she asked finally.

"What I'd call concrete proof. It showed how, when, and in what amounts Gleason had taken the money."

"This is all so confusing," Hannah said. "I just don't understand computers. How could

Gleason use this program without other people knowing it was there?"

"Easy. If someone isn't looking for a program, the odds are that it could go unnoticed for a long time," Carson said.

"Maybe if you explained the details, we'd understand this better," Nancy said.

Carson sighed. "After all these years I'm not sure I can piece it together, but I'll try." He paused. "Basically, Gleason set up a fake billing system. He took a client's bill and padded it with expenses that he added to the original amount on the bill. Then he'd send the revised bill to a client."

"And when the check came back?" Bess asked.

"The system wouldn't work with actual checks. It depends on the direct transfer of money from one bank to another. There is no way he could cash a check made out to his firm. Therefore the firm's clients transferred money from their accounts to the firm's. Any money over the amount shown on the bill would be transferred to an account Gleason had set up," Carson explained.

Bess's mouth fell open. "That's incredibly sneaky. And pretty clever, too," she added.

There was something her father had said that didn't make sense to Nancy. "How did Gleason manage to do this without Allard's knowing?" she asked.

"Good question," Carson said. "At first, he didn't do it with every client or in large amounts. But over the course of a year, he managed to collect quite a bit of money. But then he got greedy, and that was why he was caught."

"What about the money, Mr. Drew?" George asked.

"Never found. We did find the bank it had been transferred to, but it was withdrawn from that account the day before the indictments were handed down. Gleason's signature was on the check."

"What?" Nancy blinked. "It was never found? No sign that Gleason had spent any of it? They couldn't trace it to any bank account?"

Carson shook his head. "During the investigation, the district attorney tried to find the money, but it had simply disappeared." He paused. "But that's not all."

"What do you mean?" Nancy asked.

"There was a strange twist to the case," Carson began.

"What?" George asked. Bess and Hannah looked on expectantly.

"The twist was that if Gleason had told the DA where the money was he could've received a suspended sentence," Carson said.

"But he didn't," Nancy mused. "Why not?" Nancy's father leaned forward and rested his elbows on his knees. "Because he insisted right up to the end that he was innocent and that he'd been framed." Carson looked across at Nancy and waited for this last piece of news to sink in.

Nancy knew why her father had waited to tell them the most important aspect of the case. If Gleason was truly innocent, Allard might be guilty—and whoever was harassing her father could be thinking the same thing.

Carson continued. "The district attorney tried to get Gleason to tell him where the money was, but Gleason said he didn't have a clue."

"And what do you think?" Nancy wasn't going to let her father stop now.

"I'm not sure, Nancy," Carson said, rising. "But one thing I do know: It's getting late, and Bess and George ought to be heading home before their parents start to worry."

Bess took her cue. "You're right, Mr. Drew. Let's get going, George."

Bess and George went into the hallway to get their coats. After thanking Carson for dinner again, George took Nancy aside in the hallway.

"Is your dad going to be okay?" she asked. "I'm a little worried about him."

Nancy gave George a hug, then stood back and faced the cousins. "I know, guys. So am I. But between us we're going to get to the bottom of this," she said with conviction.

The phone rang, making them all jump.

Nancy reached out to grab it before Hannah or her dad could pick it up.

"Drew residence," she said into the receiver.

A sinister voice spoke slowly on the other end.

"Carson Drew defended a guilty man and got him off. I know why. And how. Now it's time for him to pay for his mistake!"

Chapter
Three

IN ONLY A SECOND Nancy had pulled herself together. Now wasn't the time to lose her cool, she thought. Not when she had the caller on the phone.

"What do you mean, you know why?" she asked, keeping her voice steady.

"He's going to pay," the voice repeated. "You tell him—"

Carson Drew must have known what was happening, because before Nancy could hear what the caller had to say, her father had pulled the phone from her hand.

"Listen," he told the caller. "If you have something to say, tell me. Otherwise, I'm going

20

to start tracing these calls and have you arrested for harassment." He slammed the phone down into its cradle.

"We should have let him talk, Dad. We might—" Nancy began.

Carson interrupted her. "Hold on," he said, facing George, Bess, Nancy, and Hannah, who were standing in a semicircle by the phone. "This isn't anything for you to worry about. You have to let me take care of this. That includes you, Nancy."

Nancy lowered her eyes and stared at a corner of the rug. When her father sounded that serious, she knew that she had to pay attention.

"But, Mr. Drew," George said, "Nancy could help you find out who's behind this."

"George, I understand why you're concerned. But chances are that if we don't take these people seriously, they'll go away. Now you should be heading home, don't you agree?"

Nancy, Bess, and George exchanged a quick look. Carson Drew obviously didn't want them getting involved. The two girls put on their coats and said good night.

After her friends had left and Hannah had gone off to bed, Nancy tried asking her father one last question. "There's one thing that still bothers me: Why do you think the money wasn't found?"

"I don't know," Carson said with a sigh. "Probably because Gleason had hidden it well —maybe in a Swiss bank account."

"But what good would it do him in jail?"

"He wouldn't be in jail forever," Carson explained. "He stole quite a bit of money, but his sentence wasn't long—five to fifteen years. He's probably out on parole by now."

Gleason would be able to use the money when he got out of prison, Nancy realized. Then another thought occurred to her. "Do you think there's any chance at all that Allard was guilty?"

"It's possible, Nancy," Carson said. A deep frown cut across his forehead. "But I honestly never found any evidence that he was. And if I had, I certainly wouldn't have suppressed it."

Nancy's father stood up and stretched. "Now I think you should go to bed. It's been a long day. And, Nancy—"

"Yes?" she asked.

"Don't even *think* that this may be a case for you to solve, okay?" he said pointedly. "In my experience, it's always better to ignore this sort of thing."

Nancy kissed her father on the cheek. "I hope you're right, Dad. Good night." But as she went upstairs to bed, Nancy resolved that this was one case she wasn't going to turn down, no matter what her father said.

* * *

Once her father had left the house the next morning, Nancy got to work. She had a lot to do.

After dressing in jeans, a peach cotton sweater, and sneakers, she called Chief McGinnis at the River Heights Police Department.

Her plan was to find out where Robert Gleason was and then go on from there. There were a few people who could know enough about the trial to make the kind of threats her father had gotten. Still, Robert Gleason was as good a person to start with as any.

"What can I help you with, Nancy?" The chief's voice came on the line after Nancy had been on hold for a short time.

"I need some information about a former client of my father's."

"What do you need to know?" McGinnis asked.

"I need his address. My father thinks he's been released on parole and wants to make sure he's got a job and all. Dad's busy, so I told him I'd help him out."

"Well, it's a little unusual." The chief paused, then asked, "What's the name?"

"Gleason. Robert Gleason." Nancy waited.

"Hold on a second. I'm looking it up on the computer. Here we are. Robert Gleason. Yep, he was released three weeks ago. His parole officer lists his address as 1476 East Main, Apartment Five-A."

Nancy recognized the address as being in one of River Heights's more run-down neighborhoods. Gleason probably wasn't doing too well.

"Thanks, Chief," Nancy said, getting ready to hang up.

"Nancy, wait a minute. I think I ought to give you a word of warning: If you just happen to be on a case and don't want to tell me because you think I might 'interfere,' you'd better come clean. Checking into a guy with a record can be tricky."

"Honestly, I'm just trying to help my father out," Nancy said.

"Okay, Nancy," he said. "I sure hope I don't find out otherwise."

Nancy smiled. She hoped so, too. "Right. Thanks again." She and Chief McGinnis had a lot of respect for each other, but he didn't always appreciate being shown up by an eighteen-year-old detective.

She quickly ran a brush through her hair. Now that she knew where to find him, she didn't want to waste any time tracking down Robert Gleason. She grabbed her jean jacket from the closet, snatched her purse from the bureau, and headed out the door.

Nancy was halfway between her house and

Robert Gleason's apartment when something Chief McGinnis had said came back to her.

Robert Gleason was released from prison three weeks earlier. The phone calls to her house had started about two weeks ago. If the two events were coincidental, it was uncanny.

As she turned down East Main, Nancy decided that Robert Gleason had the most to gain by accusing Carson Drew of withholding evidence. There was a good chance that once he was out of jail, Gleason might try to prove he was innocent.

There had to be a connection between his release and the phone calls, Nancy thought as she looked for a parking place near 1476 East Main Street.

She slammed on her brakes as she approached the building. Four police cars and an ambulance were parked right in front of it. Police officers were milling around on the sidewalk in front of the building.

As Nancy watched, the rear doors of the ambulance were yanked shut and the van pulled away from the curb and roared off, siren blaring.

Nancy walked over to the nearest police car and approached a detective whose badge read Ryan.

"What happened here?" she asked. "Some kind of accident?"

Detective Ryan looked Nancy up and down. "Not exactly. Some poor guy jumped or fell from his apartment. It looks like it probably was a suicide." He shook his head slowly. "Sad, really."

A feeling of dread washed over Nancy. "Who was it?" she asked. "Do you know his name?"

Detective Ryan glanced at Nancy with a confused expression. "You seem pretty curious about all this. Unfortunately, I have a lot to do here. You'll probably read about it in the paper." He turned and started to walk away.

Nancy followed him. "Please. I've got to know his name," she begged breathlessly.

"Okay," Detective Ryan said finally. "Since it's so important to you. His name was Gleason. Robert Gleason."

Chapter

Four

Nancy drew in a sharp breath. "Oh, no," she murmured. "It's not possible—"

Ryan reached out and put a comforting hand on Nancy's arm. "Was he a relative of yours?" he asked.

"No," Nancy answered slowly. "No, I didn't know him." She looked beyond the detective to where several police were standing guard outside Gleason's building. "Did he leave a note?" she found herself asking.

"Yes, he did," Ryan said. He gave Nancy a curious look. "Let me ask you something—if you didn't know him, why are you so interested?"

Nancy wasn't too keen on explaining what she was doing outside Gleason's building or why she wanted to know so much about him. "I was really just curious," she explained.

Ryan continued to look at her carefully. "Wait a minute," he said. "I thought I recognized you—now I know why. You're Nancy Drew, the detective, aren't you?"

"Yes, I am," Nancy said. "I was driving by, and I suppose you could say my instincts took over. If there's anything I can help with—"

"That's okay," Ryan answered with a smile. "I'd be happy for your help if I needed it, but you can leave this one to us."

Nancy could tell she wasn't going to get any more information out of Ryan, so she didn't press the point.

She slowly crossed the street and headed back to her car, thinking. Now that Robert Gleason was dead, it would be really hard to find out what connection, if any, he had to the harassment of her father. Unless . . .

She could check out his apartment for evidence. The police were probably making a sweep of the place now. Still, there was a good chance she'd find something they'd missed because they wouldn't be looking for the same things.

Several police officers were still standing in front of Gleason's building talking with Detective Ryan. He put out his arms to usher them toward the door. Now was her chance.

Nancy dashed across the street and darted around Gleason's building to the alley that ran behind it. On the back wall of the building she spied a short flight of steps that led down to a gray metal door with a single grimy window. She could just make out an elevator to the right in the basement. Lights above the elevator showed it was stopped at the fifth floor. Gleason's floor.

After trying the door and finding it locked, Nancy darted back up the stairs to look at the building to find another way in. She hadn't brought her lock-pick tools with her because she'd only planned on having a chat with Gleason, not on breaking into his building.

Looking up, Nancy saw her way in—a fire escape. All she had to do now was jump up, pull the ladder down, and make her way up the metal stairs.

Nancy pressed herself against the building and cast a quick glance around the corner to make sure no one was observing her. Then she sprung up and just reached her fingertips around a metal bar. She hung on, and her weight pulled the stairs down to the cement alley. She stole up the rusted fire escape that creaked a whining protest at each of her steps.

Within a matter of minutes Nancy was

standing outside the fifth floor window. She peered in and saw three police officers standing at the point where the two halls met. Gleason's apartment had to be down there. There was no way for her to get inside the apartment while the police were standing guard.

Nancy waited, remaining flat against the brick wall and peering in the window regularly to see if the police had gone. Finally, after twenty minutes of waiting, Nancy saw two detectives and four officers head for the back stairs that were in her view.

"It's about time," Nancy whispered to herself. She had begun to think she'd never get inside.

After allowing the officers a minute or two to go down the stairs—they didn't bother to wait for the elevator—Nancy pushed up the window and ducked into the hall.

She tiptoed quickly down the hall and around the corner to Gleason's apartment. The police had left the door open, and that meant they were coming back. She'd have to work fast.

Inside, Nancy found that her suspicions had been right. The whole place was turned upside down, leaving little or no chance of her finding anything. She scanned the threadbare apartment, taking in its few mismatched pieces of furniture and the dirty, stained rug.

She stepped into the small kitchen and

searched through the cabinets, but found only a box of cereal and two packages of spaghetti. Inside the almost bare refrigerator a cold light glowed on a quart of milk and a can of coffee.

I don't even know what I hoped to find, she thought. Still, she forced herself to continue her search. She checked under the sofa cushions, knocked on every wall for a hidden panel, and even looked inside the toilet tank. Nothing.

Finally she moved to the window that faced the street. Gleason's apartment was on a corner. One side looked out over the passageway between the buildings, but the other had a view of the street. She thought she ought to keep an eye on the activities of the police while she planned her next move.

As Nancy pulled back the frayed curtain, searching for any sign of activity below, something fell to the floor right next to her feet.

"What in the world—?" She bent down and picked up a small, red notebook. It must have been hidden on the window frame and was dislodged when she moved the curtain. Flipping the book open, she saw that it was an appointment book, with dates, names, addresses, and phone numbers written on several pages.

Before Nancy sat down to look at the book more closely, she glanced down at the street. There were no police officers in sight. That meant they had reentered the building, and Nancy had to beat it before she got caught. She slipped the book into her bag.

Her heart beating double time, Nancy stole to the door and inched it open. Peering down the hall, she saw no one, but she did hear the steady march of feet ascending the stairs. Perhaps six or seven people were closing in on the fifth floor.

Easing the door back, she slid out and tore down the hall. Head down, she barrelled around the corner and pulled up short, right against a blue serge uniform with brass buttons. She was caught!

"Hi," she managed to say.

"Hi, there, yourself," the young officer said. "Looks like you put on the brakes just in time."

Nancy smiled and said, "Looks like it." She moved slowly toward the elevator and popped in just as the first detective moved through the doorway.

As Nancy walked out the front door, her attention was drawn to a loud argument between a lone police officer and a girl and boy. They were standing just to the right of the entrance to Gleason's building.

Nancy skipped down the steps and stopped abruptly. She bent down and pretended to retie her left shoelace.

She listened as a pretty girl with long auburn hair, just about her age, spoke with the police officer. With the girl was a slightly older boy, also good-looking, dressed in an auto mechanic's uniform that didn't hide the fact that he was in great shape.

"I don't believe it," the girl was saying. "It's not possible. He couldn't have— Oh, Chris, why is this happening to us now?" She started to cry, and the boy put his arm around her shoulder and hugged her close.

"I think we'd better leave, Kate. You're not in any condition to answer questions," he said firmly.

"But I have to make them understand," the girl said tearfully. "I talked to him just a few days ago. He was happier than I can remember him being in a long time."

"You don't think your father could have killed himself?" the police officer asked her gently.

Nancy stood up and bent down again, pretending her other shoelace needed retying. These must be Robert Gleason's kids, she thought.

"That's exactly what I'm saying," the girl answered.

"Do you have any kind of proof?" the officer asked, pulling out his pad and pencil.

"What kind of proof can you give that

someone didn't kill himself? He was happy, that's all, and I know he wouldn't take his life," Kate answered.

"Kate," the boy said, quietly admonishing her. "I think the best thing would be for us to go home and let the police get on with their investigation."

As she watched the girl wipe the tears from her eyes, Nancy thought about what she had said. Apparently, Kate Gleason thought her father had been murdered. If she had a reason for thinking so, Nancy wanted to know what it was.

Nancy watched as the officer folded his notepad and slipped it into his back pocket. "Let me know if you want to make a statement," he said. Then he walked off a few feet to stand guard at the front entrance.

As soon as the boy and Kate moved off, Nancy approached them. "Sorry, but I couldn't help overhearing." Nancy turned to the boy and saw he was really good looking, with clear green eyes and thick, wavy brown hair.

"I'm really sorry about what happened," she went on. "But from what I heard you say, you think maybe your father didn't kill himself?"

The boy seemed to be ready to answer Nancy, but the girl turned on her.

"Even if we thought our father was killed,

why should we tell you?" she asked. "Who are you, anyway?"

Nancy tried to be as kind as possible. "Actually, I might be able to help you. My name is Nancy Drew, and I'm a private detective."

The girl came rushing at Nancy, screaming. "Nancy Drew! As far as I'm concerned, your father is responsible for everything that's happened. Carson Drew has my father's blood on his hands, and he's going to pay!"

Chapter

Five

"HOLD IT, KATE!" The boy moved between Nancy and Kate.

"Why should I?" Kate shouted. "What right does she have to be here, talking to us?"

Nancy found herself reeling from what Kate Gleason had said. The girl actually thought her father was to blame for Robert Gleason's death!

"You should think about what you're doing," the boy told her. Nancy heard the hint of anger in his voice.

"Don't worry, Chris," Kate said, gritting her teeth. "I wouldn't give her the satisfaction of hurting her! But she's got a lot of nerve, just the same." The girl's green eyes were half shut with fury.

"I honestly don't know what you're talking about!" Nancy said emphatically. "Don't you think you'd better explain what you mean?" she asked simply.

Kate Gleason had made a heavy accusation against her father, but Nancy knew she wouldn't find out anything if she lost her cool.

"My sister's pretty upset," Chris Gleason said. He shot Kate a serious look. "She doesn't know what she's saying."

"Thanks a lot, Chris," Kate said sarcastically. "You know as well as I do what's been going on."

As Nancy watched, Chris responded to his sister's words only with silence and a sharp look. What is it with these two? Nancy wondered.

Chris turned from his sister. "By the way, my name's Chris Gleason," the boy said, forcing a smile. "And this is my sister, Kate." Chris stuck out his right hand. Nancy shook it and turned to Kate. The girl gave Nancy a scowl and walked away.

Chris took Nancy aside. "I'm sorry about my sister," he said with a sigh. "She's taking this pretty hard."

"It's perfectly understandable," Nancy said. "It's tough losing a parent."

"Yes, it is. We didn't really know our dad all

that well because he was sent away eight years ago. But our lives have been a little rough, what with the conviction, and then my parents' divorce. And now this." He pointed to the police who were streaming out of the building now. They started to pack up and move off.

Nancy easily understood why Kate Gleason was so upset. But why, she wondered, was Chris being so nice and direct with her? Maybe the shock of his father's death hadn't sunk in yet, Nancy thought.

Kate Gleason came back over to where they were standing. "I'm glad to see you're getting along so well," she said, her upper lip curled up in a sneer. "I'd hate to have Carson Drew's daughter think we disliked her or anything."

Nancy checked her anger. Kate Gleason was being difficult, but she had just had a terrible shock. Nancy knew she had to be understanding. Besides, the Gleason kids were her only connection to Robert Gleason, and she still had a strong suspicion that he was behind that photograph and the phone call.

"I don't necessarily want you to like me," Nancy said to Kate. "And I'm really sorry about what's happened. But I think I have a right to know why you think my father's directly responsible for all of this. And," she added, "if you really think your father's death wasn't an accident, I might be able to help."

"She's right, Kate," Chris said.

Kate folded her arms. She wasn't convinced at all. Chris took her aside for a minute. Nancy heard him whispering to Kate and saw Kate looking over at her. Finally, they both came back.

"Kate's agreed to talk," Chris told Nancy. "But only because you offered to help us find out what really happened to my father."

"You're still going to have to prove to me that your father isn't actually responsible, though," Kate added.

Nancy was about to lose her temper. What right did Kate Gleason have to accuse her father of being involved in Robert Gleason's death? But Nancy knew that if she was going to get to the bottom of her father's problem, she'd also have to find a way of getting along with Kate Gleason.

"I hope that when we finish talking, you'll see you have a reason to trust me. And you'll realize we need to cooperate," Nancy said, drilling in her point.

"Maybe," Kate said grudgingly.

Nancy and Chris and Kate Gleason were sitting around a table at the Pizza Palace. They had almost finished their sodas when Nancy felt the time was right to start talking about Robert Gleason.

"Why don't you tell me what you know?" Nancy said, and took a sip of her soda. "What makes you think that your dad didn't kill himself?"

"You put it so gracefully," Kate said in a harsh voice. "Besides the fact that he was happier than ever before—nothing." Tears welled up in her eyes. "When I last talked to him he was telling me that he had a big surprise planned for my birthday. Does that sound like a man who's thinking of killing himself?"

"Not exactly," Nancy answered. "But—and I hate to say this—a lot can happen. Maybe your dad wasn't adjusting to his new life too well."

"Nancy," Chris said. "There's something Kate isn't telling you—the reason why my dad was in a better mood."

"Which was?"

"It's kind of hard to talk about, because we really don't know enough." Chris paused. "It looks like my father had new evidence about the case. Evidence he said that would 'put Dennis Allard away this time.'"

"And you think someone may have killed him because of it?" Nancy concluded gently.

"You bet we do!" Kate said, banging her fist on the table.

"But you don't know what the evidence was?" Nancy asked.

"I don't have any idea," Chris said sadly.

"Kate and I tried to get him to let us help, but he said he had to do it alone."

"But he told us that Dennis Allard framed him," Kate said. "And that your father had helped. He wouldn't let us do anything, so I—" Kate stopped.

Nancy got the distinct feeling she was about to say something important but stopped herself when she realized what she was doing.

"So you did what, Kate?" she asked pointedly.

"Nothing!" Kate shook her head and blinked back the tears that had pooled in her eyes. "All I can say is that if it hadn't been for your father, my father would never have had to prove that he was innocent. And he wouldn't be dead right now!"

Kate broke down. Before Chris could reach out to comfort her, she ran off to the bathroom.

Nancy looked at Chris. He was staring not at his sister, but at Nancy.

"Sorry," he said. "She doesn't really mean what she's saying."

"Do you think my father was responsible?" Nancy asked.

Chris sighed. "I don't know." He studied Nancy intently. Nancy returned his stare, but couldn't read him. She couldn't understand why he'd be so willing to talk to her if he thought her father had helped frame his dad.

Then, as if in answer to her question, Chris started to speak. "I think we need to trust each other," he said finally. "I want to find out who wanted my father dead, and I think you can help."

"You're right," Nancy said slowly. "I need to clear my father's name, too."

Kate Gleason came back to the table. Her eyes were red still, but she had stopped crying. "I'd like to go now," she said to her brother, making no move to sit.

"There's just one more thing I need to ask you," Nancy said. "Before you ran off, you were about to tell me something. What was it?" She focused on Kate's eyes and wouldn't look away.

"Nothing," Kate answered, finally breaking the contact.

"I don't believe you." Nancy paused. She looked across the table at Chris. "You two haven't been making phone calls to my house lately, have you?" It was only a hunch but worth a try.

Chris shook his head. Nancy looked up at Kate. Kate's eyes grew bright, and she swallowed a few times. Nancy was right!

"Kate?" Chris had seen his sister's reaction. "What's all this about?" he asked as she sat down beside him.

Nancy quickly explained about the phone calls and the photograph.

"I didn't really think about what I was doing," Kate confessed. "I wanted to help my father. I thought maybe I could scare your dad into—"

"Into what?" Nancy asked.

"I don't know." Kate rested her head in her hands, then looked up, brushing away her long auburn hair. "I thought that maybe he'd be worried enough to come clean about what he'd done," she said in a rush.

"Kate," Chris groaned. "How could you? You could have gotten into a lot of trouble. Sometimes I wonder about you."

"Look," Nancy said. "I'm not going to pretend I'm happy about what you did, but I'm glad I found out who was doing it." At least now she knew the threats weren't serious. "Still, what I don't understand—" she began.

"Then, will you help us?" Chris interrupted eagerly. "Find out who might have killed our father? And why?"

Nancy sighed. She didn't really trust Chris and Kate Gleason, but they were also too important a link to drop. "I'll help," she said finally.

For the first time since Nancy had met her, Kate Gleason acted almost kind to her.

"What's our first step?" Chris asked.

Nancy thought for a moment. "We need to find out what the evidence was that your father had. And it seems to me that the person we have to talk to is Dennis Allard. He knows more about this case than anyone."

"Allard!" Kate exclaimed. "He's the one who framed my dad in the first place! Why would he help us?"

"I don't know that Allard was guilty," Nancy said calmly. "Assuming he wasn't, he might be able to help us."

Chris nodded and silenced Kate with a stare. "I think she's right, Kate."

"Okay," Kate said with a grimace. "But I think Nancy should talk to him. I wouldn't trust myself alone with the man."

Nancy found herself smiling. "That's an excellent idea. I'll try to see him today, and I'll let you know what I find out."

The three paid their checks and left the restaurant. Outside, Nancy called information for the address of River Heights Bank and Trust, where her father had mentioned Dennis Allard now worked. Then she made sure she got the Gleasons' address and phone number before she headed downtown.

Nancy was halfway between the restaurant and the center of River Heights when she noticed that a late-model silver sports car seemed to be following her. Every time she made a turn, the car was right behind her.

Whoever was in the car had to have followed her from her house that morning. Or the driver could have seen her at Gleason's apartment building and wondered what she was up to. Either way, she wanted to lose the tail, and fast.

After making a couple of quick maneuvers in the light traffic, Nancy checked her rearview mirror again. The silver sports car was gone. She had lost it!

One quick glance in her sideview mirror told her she had decided too quickly. The car was still tailing her but was now behind two other cars.

Nancy drove for several miles more. The silver car hung back, keeping the two cars between them.

Then Nancy saw her chance. She was right by the entrance to the highway that ran along the river. Maybe once she got on the highway and picked up speed, she could lose the car and make a quick exit.

Nancy roared up the entrance ramp, with the silver car following close behind. She pushed her foot down on the accelerator. Easing ahead of the slower-moving traffic, Nancy kept her eye out for the sports car. It was still there.

An exit was coming up in the next quarter mile. Nancy planned her maneuver. An eighth of a mile to go. A sixteenth. She was almost there.

When Nancy was only twenty-five feet from the exit ramp, the sports car charged forward.

The driver had obviously been waiting for the right moment. Now the silver car was within a few feet of Nancy's Mustang.

Nancy floored the accelerator, and the sports car matched her speed and then some. The little silver car rammed into Nancy's bumper. She tried to gain control of her car, but the momentum was too much.

With one last surge, the sports car slammed into Nancy's car again. The force sent the car and Nancy flying off the road!

Chapter

Six

INSIDE HER CAR Nancy was thrown forward. But before she hit the steering wheel, Nancy saw she was flying straight for a grove of trees. If she plowed into it, she was dead.

Nancy yanked her seat belt free, wrestled the door open, and threw herself out of the car as her beloved Mustang crashed into the trees.

Whew! Nancy thought. That was about as close a call as she'd ever like to make. She pulled herself to her feet and checked to make sure she didn't have any broken bones.

Still a little wobbly and shaking inside, Nancy walked gingerly over to her car. What she saw made her very unhappy. The whole front end of the Mustang was smashed. She leaned against the wrecked car and thought.

Whoever did this knew who she was and was serious about keeping her out of action. She could easily have been killed.

Still, she couldn't let anyone stop her—especially not now. More determined than ever, she made her way back up to the highway to try to hitch a ride into town. Accident or no accident, she was going to have her little chat with Dennis Allard.

Back in the center of River Heights, Nancy called George. After her recent experience, she decided she needed help. Having Bess and George along would give Nancy another perspective when she met with Dennis Allard.

"Hello?" Nancy let out a relieved sigh when she heard George's voice on the line. At least something was going right: George was at home.

"George, it's Nancy. Listen, I need your help."

"Sure, Nancy. What's up?" George asked.

"I had a little accident—"

"What happened?" George interrupted. "Are you all right?"

Nancy tried to keep her voice calm. She didn't want to worry her friend. "I'm fine. If you pick me up, I'll explain everything."

"Where are you?" Nancy gave her the address of the gas station where she had gone to arrange to have her car towed.

"Please bring Bess along. I've got an errand to run and I'd appreciate your help."

"No problem. We'll be there in ten minutes." George said goodbye and hung up.

Nancy wandered over to the mechanic who was checking out her car. It had just been lowered off the tow truck.

"It's not going to be cheap," he said, shaking his head.

"I think you're probably right," Nancy said. "How long is it going to take to fix it?"

"Depends. Probably we'll have to wait for the parts. I'd say you'll be living without it for at least two weeks."

The mechanic looked Nancy over for the first time, taking in her dusty jeans and grass-stained sweater. "You don't look so good yourself. You sure you're okay?"

Nancy smiled wanly. "I'm sure," she said. "But I guess I could use a little cleaning up."

Nancy headed for the restroom. There she wiped off her jeans and decided to put on a jacket to hide the worst stains. After combing her hair, fixing her eye makeup, and putting on a fresh coat of lip gloss, she decided she looked respectable enough to see Dennis Allard.

Within a few minutes George swung into the gas station.

"What's going on?" Bess asked, leaning forward to let Nancy into the backseat. She had seen the smashed Mustang parked nearby.

"Someone ran me off the road," Nancy explained.

George let out a whistle. "When did that happen?"

"Just an hour ago." She gave George the address of the River Heights Bank and Trust. "Let's get going. I want to see Dennis Allard. I'll tell you all about it on the way over."

During the ride Nancy told Bess and George about her morning with Chris and Kate Gleason, and her run-in with the silver sports car.

"Sounds like someone doesn't want you to get too close," George said when Nancy had finished.

"I think you're right," Nancy agreed.

"Any idea who it could be?" Bess asked.

Nancy shook her head. "Not yet. That's part of the reason I want to meet with Allard."

"I don't get it, Nan," Bess said as George parked the car in front of Allard's bank. "Why do you think he can help?"

Nancy waited until they were out of the car to answer. "I'm not sure I can trust Chris and Kate. I get the feeling there's something they're not telling me.

"And I don't know who really is innocent. Meanwhile, Allard does know the case inside and out, so maybe he can give me some idea of what kind of person Robert Gleason really was."

"Good thinking," George said as they headed for the bank.

Within a few minutes, Nancy, Bess, and George were sitting in Dennis Allard's office. Nancy broke the news about Robert Gleason's death as gently as possible. The two had worked together, and she didn't know how upset Allard might get.

"I always knew he was unstable," Dennis Allard said. "But I would never have predicted . . ." He didn't finish the sentence.

Nancy looked at the man carefully. He was even more handsome in person than in his photograph. His nearly black hair had a touch of gray at the temples, and there were only the beginnings of lines around his startlingly blue eyes. Allard's navy pinstripe suit fit neatly over his athletic body.

"How well did you know Gleason?" Nancy asked. "Did he seem like the type to—"

"Never," Allard said, guessing at what Nancy would say. "But I didn't know him all that well. We worked together at the law firm for about a year before the lawsuit." Allard paused for a second, then rubbed his cheek.

Nancy, Bess, and George waited expectantly for Allard to continue.

"There is one thing that might help you," he went on. "When the job of senior accountant came up, Gleason was sure that he'd get the promotion."

"What happened?" George asked.

"The firm gave it to me instead," he said, shaking his head ruefully. "Gleason wasn't too thrilled. He seemed to have been counting on it."

"Do you think he held a grudge against you?" Nancy asked.

"He certainly seemed to. When the case came to trial, he tried all kinds of ways to pin the blame on me."

"But from what Nancy's dad said, it was pretty clear he did it," Bess said.

Allard smiled. "Luckily, justice was served." He looked at Nancy. "I'm very grateful to your father for what he did. It was only because of his defense that I was able to preserve my career."

Nancy stood up, ready to leave. "There's just one more question," she said.

"Yes?" Allard asked.

"What do you think happened to the money? It was never found, you know."

"It is strange, don't you think?" George put in.

"Yes, it is," Allard said with a nod. "But my theory is that Gleason hid it away very carefully. He was probably going to claim it soon."

"That's what Mr. Drew thinks, too," Bess said.

Nancy shook Allard's hand and thanked him for answering their questions.

"I wish I could have helped more," Allard said, showing them out of his office. "But in all honesty, I try not to think about that case. It nearly ruined my life."

Now it might ruin my father's, Nancy thought. "Thanks for your help," she said, ushering Bess and George into the hall. "We'll let you get back to work."

"So what do you think, Nan?" George asked. The three friends were sitting in the Drews' living room, looking at the red date book. They had just returned from renting Nancy a car.

"I don't know," Nancy said, shaking her head. "Nothing in here tells me anything." She closed the book and started to talk. "Allard seems honest enough, but he could be playing it cool to see what happens."

"What I don't understand is why Robert Gleason would have killed himself, if he knew where the money was," Bess pointed out.

Carson Drew walked into the living room. "What's this about Robert Gleason?" he asked.

"He died this morning, Dad. He may have committed suicide," Nancy said quietly.

53

A shocked look passed over Carson's face. "That's terrible," he murmured softly. "How do you know?"

Nancy explained about her trip to Gleason's building. She was about to tell him about her conversation with Chris and Kate Gleason, but she stopped because her father seemed preoccupied.

"What is it, Dad?" she asked. "You're hardly listening."

Carson sauntered over to the front window and looked out. "It's just that this is all so awful."

Nancy exchanged a look with Bess and George, then went over to her father. "There's something you're not telling me, isn't there?"

Carson took a deep breath, then abruptly he spoke up. "Did you see *Today's Times?*" he asked.

Nancy shook her head. Carson left the living room and came back in a minute carrying the River Heights newspaper. Nancy took it from her father.

"Read page two," he said.

After Nancy opened the paper, Bess and George stood and read over her shoulder. She scanned the page to find out what her father was talking about.

Then she saw it. A small column at the bottom of the page carried a headline, "DA Promises to Reopen Case." She skimmed the story. Her father's name leapt out at her, along with the words *suppressing evidence* and *tampering*.

Nancy couldn't bring herself to read the whole story. "What does this mean?" she asked. George and Bess looked at Carson expectantly.

"Exactly what it says. The district attorney is threatening to reopen the case against Dennis Allard."

"But he can't do that!" Nancy said. "Can he?" she added weakly.

"He seems to think he can," Carson said.

"On what grounds?" George asked.

Carson waited, then took a deep breath. "He's going to bring charges against me for obstructing justice!"

Chapter

Seven

That's got to be the most ridiculous thing I've ever heard," George said. "No one would believe you'd obstruct justice!"

Nancy watched as her father managed a small smile. She couldn't believe this was happening. "Thanks for the vote of confidence, George," Carson said.

"You have mine, too, Mr. Drew," Bess added, putting her hand on his arm. Then she turned to her cousin. "I think you and I should go, George. We'll see you later, Nan."

Nancy followed them to the front door and out to George's car, in the driveway.

"I wish there were something we could do, Nancy," Bess said, slipping into the passenger seat.

"I do, too," Nancy answered. "But I've got to find out what's going on, and why."

"Let me guess," George said, leaning over Bess. "You were thinking you might just be able to help your father if you could talk to the district attorney."

"I guess we've known each other too long." Nancy smiled. "I *would* like to know why he's doing this. And who put him up to it."

"Don't get in over your head, and call us if you need help," George said as she put her car into reverse, getting ready to back out of the Drews' driveway.

"Don't worry about me," Nancy said. "I'll be all right. It's my father I'm worried about." With that, she headed back inside.

Carson Drew was on the phone, and Nancy could hear only his end of the conversation.

"I'll do that," he was saying. "No, I don't think it's necessary. Fine. Call me tomorrow."

"Who was that, Dad?" Nancy asked.

"A colleague of mine. I thought I'd better call him," Carson answered.

"Dad, this is more serious than you're letting on, isn't it?"

Nancy saw her father hesitate before he answered her. There were lines of worry around his eyes and mouth. It wasn't the first time he had tried to protect her or prevent her from getting involved in a case. But it would be worse than maddening if he wouldn't let her help him this time. It could be disastrous.

"You've got to let me help you," she began. "I can't just sit still while someone tries to destroy your career."

Carson Drew went over to his daughter and placed his hands on her shoulders. "I know you want to help," he said, "but there's nothing you can do. If the district attorney wants to reopen the case, he can if he has enough evidence to support his claims."

"And does he?" Nancy asked.

"I don't know. I'm not even sure what he's basing his accusations on. But there's got to be something. If only I knew what it was . . ."

Carson stepped away from Nancy and sat down on the couch. He leaned over, rested his elbows on his knees, and clasped his hands together.

"Please, Dad," Nancy begged, "you've got to let me help you. There must be something we can do." She thought for a moment. "Who might have gone to the DA? He wouldn't have thought to reopen this case on his own, would he?"

Carson shook his head. "The only person who knows enough about the trial is Gleason's former lawyer, Edward Vaughn. But I don't see why he would have—"

"Why not?" Nancy asked excitedly. "What if Gleason had gone back to him, claiming to have evidence to prove that he was innocent?"

"What sort of evidence?" Carson asked curiously.

"I don't know." Nancy then explained what Chris and Kate Gleason had told her. "So maybe Gleason really had come up with something that showed Allard was guilty in the first place," she concluded. "Would that be enough for Gleason's lawyer—what's his name, Vaughn?"

Carson nodded.

Nancy went on. "Would Vaughn go to the district attorney with the information?"

Carson narrowed his eyes and thought for a moment. "It's possible," he said. "But only if he had real proof. He wouldn't risk his career for less."

Nancy pointed to the article. "But from what this says, the DA's only *threatening* to reopen the case. All I read is 'alleged' and 'looking into the possibility.' It looks like this reporter's basing his story on some kind of leak."

"You're right, Nancy." Carson sighed, reading the story again. "There's nothing here that says he's got proof."

"That means there's a chance we can fight this!" Nancy said emphatically.

"Listen to me, Nancy," Carson said, putting a hand on her shoulder. "There's nothing you can do."

Nancy tried to interrupt. "But, Dad—"

Her father stopped her. "Please. We're going to have to wait and see what happens. And I'd better not find out that you've gotten any more involved than you already are. This is one case you shouldn't even think of solving. Do you understand?"

Nancy gave up. "Sure, I understand." It hurt her a bit that her father didn't think she could help, but she knew how stubborn he could be.

"Thanks, Nancy," Carson said with a sad smile. "I know how hard this must be for you."

"Not any harder than it is for you," Nancy answered wearily, picking up the date book and carrying it upstairs.

The next morning Nancy stood in a plush reception room, waiting to see Edward Vaughn. All night she had thought about what her father had said. Normally, she would have followed his advice. Then she decided that if she managed to help her father, he'd have no choice but to forgive her for not listening to him.

"Mr. Vaughn's secretary says you should make an appointment and come back," the receptionist said, interrupting Nancy's thoughts.

"Did you tell him it's important?" she asked.

The receptionist eyed Nancy. Obviously she didn't appreciate a teenager telling her how to do her job.

"Of course I told him, Ms. Drew, but he's a very busy man. Now I have to get back to work." At least five lights were blinking on the phone console. "Good morning, Stein and Daly, please hold. Good morning, Stein and Daly, please hold."

Nancy saw her chance to slip past the receptionist and down the firm's bustling corridor. Vaughn didn't want to see her, but she had to talk to him, and she was going to find a way to do it.

She asked the first person she saw to direct her to Vaughn's office. Following the instructions, Nancy made a left at the first corner and saw Vaughn's nameplate on the second door on her right.

Through the open office door, she caught a glimpse of Vaughn. He was busy talking on the phone and taking notes on a large yellow legal pad.

"Can I help you?" Nancy turned to see a thin, blond-haired woman dressed in a gray suit stand up from her desk.

"Um, yes," Nancy answered. "Could you

see if Mr. Vaughn can take a minute to talk to me?" She waited while the woman, who was not much older than she, looked her up and down. She was clearly a pro, despite her age, at screening visitors.

"The receptionist must have told you that Mr. Vaughn is very busy," the woman said in a cold voice.

"What's going on out here, Pam?" Edward Vaughn was standing in his doorway. Although he was short and kind of pudgy, Vaughn was an intimidating presence. "Who are you?" he asked, looking at Nancy.

"Mr. Vaughn, my name's Nancy Drew, and I'd like to talk to you." Nancy tried to appear confident. She hoped her name would catch his attention. It did.

"Nancy Drew. Are you related to Carson Drew?" he asked.

"I'm his daughter," Nancy admitted.

"Well," Vaughn said, dragging the word out. He took his hands out of his pockets and reached out to shake Nancy's hand. "Pleased to meet you, Nancy Drew. Why don't you come in?"

That was easy, Nancy thought. But why is he being so nice to me all of a sudden? She followed him into his office, her guard up.

Vaughn motioned to a comfortable leather armchair. "Have a seat. Now what could have made you want to come to see me?" He walked around his desk and sat down. Before Nancy could answer, he spoke again.

"Let me guess." Vaughn leaned back in his chair and wove his hands together behind his head. "Could it have something to do with a case the district attorney's about to bring against your father?" His tone was arrogant. "You know, you shouldn't even be here. I doubt your father would approve."

Nancy began to wonder if she might be out of her element. She realized in a flash that a conversation with a lawyer who was probably pressing charges against her own father could be a serious conflict of interest. But there was no going back now.

"He doesn't know I'm here," she said. "And I'd appreciate it if you didn't tell him. But it's not what you think. I'm not here to ask you about his case. Actually, I thought you might be able to give me some background information on Robert Gleason."

"Robert Gleason. Now why do you want to know about him?" A frown crept over Vaughn's face.

"Did you know he committed suicide?" Nancy asked.

"Yes." Vaughn moved forward in his chair and leaned his elbows on his desk. "His son called me yesterday. A real tragedy."

"I think Gleason may have known something about his trial," Nancy ventured, "something about evidence from that trial." She paused, then plunged in. "I was wondering if you had any idea what that might be."

"Nancy Drew." Vaughn laughed. Then he took a puff from a cigar that lay in an ashtray on his desk. "You obviously don't know much about the law. As Gleason's lawyer I'm not allowed to tell you anything about that trial. Or about evidence that did or did not exist at that time or now."

"But Gleason may have been killed because of it. Doesn't that mean anything to you?" Nancy sensed a note of desperation creeping into her voice. She tried to remain calm.

Vaughn looked at her intently. "Look, I can't tell you anything about the trial that you don't already know. If you've talked to your father about it, you know as much as there is to know." He stood up. "I think you'd better go now."

"Mr. Vaughn, please." Nancy grabbed at a straw. "We both want the same thing."

"How's that?"

"You've obviously been in touch with the Gleason kids," she said quickly. "I can tell they're behind your wanting to bring the case up again, right?"

"And if they are?" Vaughn looked at Nancy seriously for the first time.

"Then we should work together, not separately. If there's evidence to prove that Gleason was innocent, I want to find it, too." She had to make him understand. "It's the only way I can prove that my father didn't have anything to do with hiding something in the original trial."

Vaughn stepped around his desk and closed his office door, which had been open the whole time they were talking. He turned to face Nancy.

"I'll do one thing for you, Ms. Drew. I'll arrange an appointment for you at Gleason's old firm. You can talk to Peter Nicodemus, the director of administration there. That's as far as I'll go, and don't ask me why I'm even doing that."

Nancy breathed a sigh of relief. She had gotten somewhere, at least. She couldn't believe her luck. "Thank you. You don't know what a help this is," she said.

"I don't know what you hope to find out there," Vaughn said. "But I'm only doing this on one condition."

"Which is?" Nancy asked.

"Whatever you find will have to become evidence for the DA's case against Carson Drew. You could be put up on the stand." Vaughn gave her a hard look.

"The DA's case." The words rang in Nancy's ears. Then she realized what Vaughn was saying.

He was telling her she could end up as a witness for the prosecution, testifying against her own father!

Chapter

Eight

BUT—" NANCY SAID. She was in shock.

Vaughn crossed the room and sat on the edge of his desk, facing Nancy.

"Let me explain. If you talk to Nicodemus, you could very well find evidence that furthers our case against your father," he said.

"Except that you won't tell me what that case is," Nancy said, regaining her composure.

"I can't. That would be a violation of ethics," Vaughn concluded.

Nancy shook herself. "That's an unfair position to put me in," she said weakly.

"That may be true. But now that you've

talked to me, we have the right to subpoena your testimony," Vaughn told her. "That means that no matter how you get in to see Nicodemus, we can call you to trial and force testimony out of you. There's nothing to protect you from that happening."

Nancy met Vaughn's eyes and considered her options. What did she hope to find out from Nicodemus anyway? His personal opinions about Robert Gleason and Dennis Allard more than anything else. And what was Vaughn's angle? What did he have on her father?

Nancy realized the mess she had gotten herself into.

"I'll see Nicodemus," she concluded, standing up and slinging her purse over her shoulder. "And I understand what you're telling me. But I'm not going to report back to you about what I learn from him unless I think it will help my father."

"I didn't think you would," Vaughn said. "And I'm not asking you to. But I wouldn't be doing my job if I didn't warn you." He stood up and walked over to reach for the doorknob. The interview was at an end.

As Nancy was leaving she turned in the doorway and tried one last question. "Just what kind of proof do you have? I'm sure you know how serious it is to go to the DA and accuse my father of obstructing justice."

"I haven't accused Carson Drew of anything. Yet," Vaughn said.

"Pam, call Peter Nicodemus," he called past Nancy out the door. "The number's in the Rolodex. Tell him that I'm sending Nancy Drew over and that he should give her a royal tour."

Nancy asked Vaughn for Nicodemus's address, and since it wasn't far, she decided to walk. It would give her time to think.

Nancy left the building, only vaguely aware of the people around her. She was lost in thought. Vaughn must have some important piece of evidence against her father, or at the least he must think he did. She might find out what it was from Mr. Nicodemus, but probably not, since Vaughn had agreed to send her there.

So who's holding the key? she wondered. Had Gleason contacted Vaughn before he died? Was there something Chris and Kate Gleason weren't telling her?

Before she knew it, Nancy was taking the elevator up to Mobley and Myerson's offices on the fifteenth floor of an elegant brick building. To her right were glass doors and a brass plaque with the company name. She took a deep breath and pushed on the brass doorplate.

Nancy had barely announced herself to the receptionist when a tall, handsome man wandered out to the firm's reception area. She was startled to see how young he was. If it hadn't been for a few gray hairs, she would have taken Peter Nicodemus for a college student.

"Nancy Drew," Nicodemus said, greeting her with his right hand extended. "I'm glad I've finally gotten a chance to meet Carson Drew's daughter and River Heights's most famous detective."

Nancy took his hand and shook it. "Nice to meet you," she said.

"I guess we should start on this floor," Nicodemus was saying. "This is where most of the attorneys work. Except, of course, for the partners. They have their own floor just above this one."

Nancy followed Nicodemus as he led the way down the firm's halls. Along the outside wall, lawyers had their offices. Each one had at least one large window, and each one's furniture and decoration reflected a slightly different personality. On the inside wall, across from the lawyers' offices, secretaries sat at desks behind chest-high partitions.

"If you'll come this way, I'll show you the nuts and bolts of the operation." Nicodemus led her down a flight of stairs. By the time they reached the next floor, Nancy noticed the noise level had increased considerably.

They were in one large room, separated by partitions that went halfway up to the ceiling.

At the far end of the large space was a sort of secretarial pool, except that all the employees there were at computer terminals instead of typewriters.

"This is our word-processing department. All the firm's work goes in and out of here at some point," Nicodemus explained.

"And over here," he said, pointing to an area close to them, "is the accounting department. That was why you came, right?"

"Yes," she answered. "I wanted to know about Robert Gleason and Dennis Allard, the two accountants who worked here and were accused of embezzling from the firm." It was an abrupt remark, but it didn't seem to faze Nicodemus.

"That was the most, well—embarrassing thing that could ever have happened to the firm." Nicodemus shook his head. "And for me, too."

"Why is that?" Nancy asked.

"I was the manager of accounting at the time, and it was all going on under my nose." Nicodemus glanced around to make sure no one was listening. "I handled the whole situation pretty effectively once I found out. At least the firm was pleased. That's part of the reason why they promoted me to director of administration."

"Is there anyone else still in the department who would remember Gleason or Allard?"

Nancy asked as Nicodemus guided her across the room. Soon they were standing in the middle of a row of desks where bookkeepers' fingers danced quickly across calculators.

"I'm afraid not," he said. "We let most of the staff go." Nancy gave him a surprised look. "I know it seems harsh, but we had to. There was no way of telling who else might have been involved in some small way."

Another dead end, Nancy thought, but she wasn't ready to give up yet. "Could you give me a list of who was working here at the time?"

"Sure." Nicodemus smiled softly. "I'll have my secretary make one up."

Nancy had noticed there wasn't much privacy in the accounting area. "How do you think Gleason managed it?" she asked. "The embezzlement."

"I know it seems improbable, but essentially there were no safeguards," Nicodemus explained. "He was in charge of one aspect of the firm's accounting and Allard, the other. He phonied the accounts so well that even I didn't recognize his scheme." Nicodemus nervously ran his hands through his curly black hair at the memory of it.

"But things have changed here," he went on. "We rearranged the whole department. One person inputs the billing information. Another goes over it to make sure it matches the computer files. And the data manager keeps track of the files, cleaning out old copies and double-checking that the person who input the information got it right."

Nancy could see from all the activity in the room that the new system kept everyone pretty busy. Then she had a thought.

"Can I talk to the data manager? There might be something in the old files that has to do with the case," she explained.

Nicodemus looked at her carefully. "But the police and the district attorney looked at all those records. More than once. I don't think you're going to find anything."

Nancy knew he was probably right. "Even so," she said. "I'd like to take a look."

"Sure." Nicodemus walked over to a corner of the room where a woman sat in front of a computer screen, a stack of printouts piled high on her desk.

"Cheryl Pomeroy, meet Nancy Drew. Nancy would like to ask you some questions about our computer records."

The girl in charge was only a few years older than Nancy, and from the way she responded to Nicodemus, Nancy could tell she was more than a little intimidated by him. She pushed her cropped black hair behind her ears, then fidgeted with the collar of her white shirt.

"What did you want to know?" Cheryl asked finally.

"Do you know about the embezzlement that happened here at the firm?" Nancy began.

Cheryl nodded. "Everyone does. It's the first office gossip you hear," she said, smiling a little. Then she got serious again and stared at Nancy with huge gray eyes.

"What I'm interested in is any old files that date from that time. Have you seen anything on the computer records that goes back that far?"

"I only started a few weeks ago." Cheryl stopped and looked up at Nicodemus, who nodded for her to go ahead. Now Nancy knew why the girl was so timid. It was probably her first job.

"And?" Nancy tried to be gentle with her questions.

"From what I understand, the DA subpoenaed all those records. They were carted out of here, including all the printouts," Cheryl said.

"Haven't you ever found anything they might have missed?" Nancy prodded.

Cheryl shook her head. "Some of the files go back that far, and I've been weeding them out. But, no, I don't remember seeing a file that had to do with the embezzlement."

"I hope you don't mind my asking, but how can you be sure?" Nancy asked politely.

"I would have recognized the list of clients," she explained, looking up at Nicodemus. "Everyone around here knows who they were."

Nicodemus looked at Nancy. "I'm sorry we can't help you," he said. He glanced at his watch. "I'm afraid I have to get back to work now. It's getting late."

Nancy looked up at the clock; it was nearly three in the afternoon and she hadn't had lunch yet. She decided to head home to wait for her father. He'd told her he might leave work early.

Nicodemus ushered her out of the department and left her at the bank of elevators. "I hope you aren't too disappointed," he said, pushing the down button. "But that case is ancient history."

Nancy stepped into the elevator just then. "Thanks anyway," she said as the doors slid shut.

Nancy had only been back home for a few minutes when the doorbell rang.

She rushed out of the kitchen with an "I'll get it" to Hannah. When she opened the door, Nancy was astonished. Cheryl Pomeroy was standing on the Drews' front porch.

"I'm sorry to bother you," Cheryl said. "Can I come in?"

75

"Sure." Nancy held the door open, confusion on her face. She wondered how Cheryl had found her.

Cheryl must have read her face well because she answered Nancy's unspoken question. "I left work early and followed you. I had to. I just couldn't keep quiet any longer."

"About what? What's wrong? Did something happen at work?"

"No. Well, yes." Cheryl suddenly broke down into tears.

"Cheryl, what's the matter?" Nancy asked.

"I'm not sure how to say this. A few weeks ago Robert Gleason was at the firm, in our department."

"And?"

"And he asked the same sort of questions you were asking today," she said ominously.

Nancy put her hand out on the girl's arm. "I don't understand. Take it easy and explain."

"Don't you see?" Cheryl asked. There was an edge of desperation in her voice. "It's just too much."

"What is, Cheryl?" Nancy asked patiently.

"He wanted to know about the files, too. I let him borrow one." She drew in a deep breath. "Now he's dead! Oh, Nancy, what's going to happen to *me* if someone finds out what I did?"

Chapter

Nine

CHERYL POMEROY BROKE DOWN and started to sob. Nancy put her arms around the girl and walked her into the kitchen. Hannah was in there, starting to prepare dinner. She raised a questioning eyebrow at Nancy when she saw Cheryl.

"I'll explain later," Nancy whispered to Hannah. She turned back to Cheryl.

The girl was fingering a wadded-up piece of tissue, but she had stopped crying. She sat down at the Drews' kitchen table.

"I just want to get this whole thing off my chest," she said, cupping her chin in her hands.

"Ever since it happened, I've been afraid someone would find out what I did."

"What do you mean, what you did?" Nancy asked soothingly, sitting down next to Cheryl.

"You have to understand. I could lose my job. It's my first—I only graduated in June from junior college. Already I've made a mistake that could cost me my job."

Nancy reached out and put a hand on Cheryl's shoulder. "Take it easy," she said. "I wouldn't tell anyone, if that's what's worrying you."

"It wouldn't matter if you did. I've already gotten in too deep." Cheryl looked as if she was on the verge of tears again.

Hannah coughed. Nancy remembered she hadn't explained what this was all about, but now wasn't the time. "Hannah—" she began.

"You don't have to ask," Hannah said. "I can see you want to be alone. I have some things to do upstairs, anyway."

"Thanks," Nancy said, smiling.

As soon as Hannah had left, Nancy turned back to Cheryl. "Now, why don't you start at the beginning. Robert Gleason came to see you?" she asked, trying to keep the girl going.

"Not me," Cheryl answered, sniffing. "He must have come to see Mr. Nicodemus. But somehow he got down into my department and started nosing around."

"What was he looking for?" Nancy asked.

"I didn't know at first. When he found out I was in charge of the computer records he started asking me all sorts of questions. The same kind of questions you were asking me today."

That explained why Cheryl had been so scared earlier, Nancy realized. She began to put the pieces together. "And you found something that would help him, right?" she asked encouragingly.

Cheryl nodded. "At first I decided not to help him. I should have followed my first impulse."

Cheryl got up and began pacing around the kitchen. "But he seemed like such a nice man, and I couldn't believe all those things people had said about him."

"So you decided to trust him?" Nancy asked.

"In the end I didn't have any choice. I let it slip that I had found a file in the computer records that had both his and Dennis Allard's names on it."

Nancy was excited but confused. "I thought you said all the files were gone."

"I didn't tell the truth." Cheryl paused. "I didn't want Mr. Nicodemus to know."

"I understand," Nancy said, nodding. "Then everything would have come out. But tell me, how did you find it?"

Cheryl took a deep breath. "It was buried

deep in the computer—all the way back in files from eight years ago," she explained. "Actually, I had found it by accident—I typed in a wrong code—but it was the right one for me to get access to that program. As I said, it was completely accidental."

Nancy edged closer. "Go on," she said. "Gleason asked you for the file—"

"He did more than ask." Cheryl's gray eyes grew large at the memory. "He wouldn't leave me alone. He started talking loudly, demanding the file, and pretty soon I realized that people were looking at us. So to quiet him down, I accessed it and gave him a copy."

Cheryl placed her hands on the table next to Nancy and leaned over them. Tears were making their way down her cheeks. "You have to understand, I didn't know what I was doing. He kept saying he was innocent and he needed the file to prove it. I didn't know what else to do."

"I know you didn't." Nancy stood up and put her arm around Cheryl. "Try not to get so upset."

"Hi, Nancy. What's going on?" Carson Drew stood in the doorway to the kitchen, taking in Cheryl and Nancy.

"Dad, this is Cheryl Pomeroy. She's got some important information about Robert Gleason."

Cheryl nodded to Carson, then sat down again while Nancy explained to her father what had happened.

"I thought I had very specifically asked you not to get involved," Carson said sternly.

Nancy tried her best to make her father understand. "You did, but I had to do something." She had left out the part about seeing Vaughn—that, she'd explain later.

"Well, what's done is done. Right now we have to deal with Cheryl." Carson turned to the girl. "What do you think was in the file you gave Gleason?" he asked gently.

"That's what's so confusing," she answered, looking at Carson. "The file was divided into twelve parts, one for every month of the year. It had to be a copy of the firm's books."

"For what year?" Nancy asked.

"The same year the embezzling occurred."

"You're sure?" Carson asked.

Cheryl nodded. "I checked. And what was really strange was that when I went to double-check the figures with the firm's books, they were all different." She wrinkled her forehead. "It just doesn't make sense," she concluded.

It made sense to Nancy and Carson. "What made Gleason so excited was that he knew you had found a copy of the phony set of books!" she said.

"Wait a minute, Nancy," Carson said. "Why

would that help him? He knew we all had a copy of the faked records. They were what convicted him in the first place."

"What good would it do Gleason to have another copy of the evidence that had sent him to jail?"

"But you said that Gleason practically begged you for a copy, right?" Nancy asked Cheryl.

The girl nodded sadly. "And—this is the worst part—he asked me to delete the file from the system. He said that he didn't want anyone else getting their hands on what he had." She moaned. "I can't believe I did it. If it was really that important, I probably did the worst thing someone with my job could ever do. It's like destroying evidence."

Nancy saw her father flinch. "Can you remember anything else about the file?" she asked.

"Nothing. I've told you everything I know." She picked up her purse and smiled.

Nancy studied Cheryl for a moment. Her mood had changed a lot from the scared girl who had been sitting there just a few minutes ago. Now she seemed in control, almost relieved.

"I'm really glad I told you about all this," Cheryl said. "But as I said, if anyone finds out I could lose my job. So—"

"I'm not going to tell anyone," Nancy assured her. "Thanks for your help."

Nancy let Cheryl out and watched as she got in her car. Carson was standing in the living room when she came back inside.

"I know what you're going to say," Nancy said. "That I shouldn't have done what I did. But I couldn't just stand by and do nothing."

"Nancy," Carson said. "From now on, you do have to leave this alone. The district attorney will take care of it."

"You're right." Nancy reached into the hall closet for her coat.

"Where are you going now?" Carson asked.

"Don't look so suspicious," Nancy said with a smile. "I promised George I'd meet her." She put on her coat, gave her father a peck on the cheek, and left the house.

She hadn't promised George at all. But as Nancy started her rental car, she didn't stop to think about it. She wanted to follow Cheryl. There was something wrong here, and she was going to find out what it was.

She picked out Cheryl's car as it turned the corner. After a few minutes Nancy realized that Cheryl was driving in the direction of Robert Gleason's apartment. Sure enough, Cheryl stopped her car right in front of the building.

Nancy waited a minute for Cheryl to get

inside, then followed her upstairs. She listened outside Gleason's apartment. There were voices inside—a man's and Cheryl's.

"It's got to be here somewhere," Nancy heard the man say. There was the sound of furniture being moved and scraped over the floor. Suddenly Cheryl was shouting, and Nancy heard glass breaking.

There wasn't any time to waste. Nancy turned the knob and pushed against the door. It moved only a couple of inches. The door was being held by a light chain.

Cheryl's voice and the man's grew louder, and Nancy could tell their fight was becoming heated.

Nancy nudged her shoulder up against the door and pushed up and in at the same time with one great burst. The chain popped. Nancy stepped in. What she saw made her freeze for a second.

Chris Gleason had Cheryl Pomeroy up against the wall. His hands were moving up toward her throat.

It looked as if he was going to strangle her!

Chapter

Ten

"Stop!" Nancy cried. Chris was so startled that he dropped his hands and took a step back.

He tripped over Nancy, who had rushed up to him, and landed flat on his back. From a seated position, he glared up at her before pulling himself to his feet.

"You'll be sorry," he said in a flat, ominous tone. Then, before Nancy could stop him, he ran out of the apartment, slamming the door behind him.

"Are you okay?" Nancy asked Cheryl.

Cheryl rubbed her throat and took a deep breath. "I think so."

Nancy ran to the window in time to see Chris climb into his car. Within a few seconds, he had his headlights on and was speeding off.

Cheryl ran over to Nancy, pulled back the curtain, and watched as the red taillights winked out on Chris's car as he sped down the deserted street.

"I don't know what's happened to him," she said, bursting into tears. "I've never seen him like this before. He seems to be possessed!"

Was there something going on between Cheryl Pomeroy and Chris Gleason? Nancy wondered.

"Are you and Chris dating?" Nancy asked, searching Cheryl's face.

Cheryl nodded silently. She turned and stared out the window; then, with a sigh, she started talking.

"He made me promise not to tell you," she said softly. "He said I shouldn't trust you. That's what got him so angry—that I went to see you."

Nancy drew in a sharp breath. "He was going to attack you just because you visited me?" she asked gently.

"As I said, he's changed a lot. But I don't think he would have actually hurt me." Nancy saw uncertainty pass over Cheryl's clear gray eyes. "He used to be such a nice guy, but now he's gotten so serious. Maybe it's because of his father. I don't know. But I can't keep any of this to myself anymore. Oh, Nancy, what should I do?"

Nancy reached over and put an arm around Cheryl's shoulders. "I'm sure he's going through a tough time," she said. "Everything will work out."

"You think so?" Cheryl's face brightened.

"I do," Nancy answered.

"I hope you're right, because he's the reason I helped Robert Gleason."

Nancy knew she should have guessed. The case was getting more complicated by the minute.

"Now he doesn't seem to care about what I've already done for him," Cheryl went on breathlessly. "He just keeps asking me more and more questions. What was in the file. Can't I get another copy. He won't let up." The story was spilling out of Cheryl. "I'm telling you, he's driving me crazy!"

"I'll bet he is," Nancy said sympathetically. She didn't want Cheryl to stop now. Finally, she felt she was getting some real clues. "You feel as if he's using you," she said.

"Exactly," Cheryl said. "And he won't let go of this thing. He says he's convinced that someone killed his dad for that evidence. He says that if he can just find it, he'll prove his father was innocent. But in the back of my mind I wonder if he isn't after money, too."

"What makes you think that?" Nancy felt herself getting close to what was making Chris Gleason act so crazy.

"Because he went to visit Dennis Allard and because I know his mother doesn't have much," Cheryl said. "He had to drop out of college because he couldn't afford it. Now he's working as a foreign-car mechanic, and all he talks about is how important it is to find the money."

"Cheryl, I do think I have to agree with you. Chris Gleason may not care as much about his father's innocence as he claims."

A look of fear spread over Cheryl's face. "I know what you're thinking. You're thinking that Chris cares about nothing *but* the money. But he isn't like that. I know he wants to prove his dad innocent, too."

"But he is definitely on the trail of the missing money, and he is using us to help him find it," Nancy said.

Cheryl put her hands over her ears, as if she were blocking out Nancy's words. "I don't believe he's using me," she said desperately.

Nancy could see that Cheryl was too confused to think clearly. It couldn't be easy to face those kinds of facts about a guy you cared about a lot. Nancy decided to go easy.

"Okay." She paused, thinking. "Let's say Chris cares most about proving his father innocent, and he's only trying to find the money because he thinks that will help set the record straight."

"I'm sure that's it," Cheryl said quickly. "I know Chris, and I think that that's what's going on in his mind."

"Then what you've got to do is convince him that I'm really on his side and want to help him," Nancy said. "Can you do that?"

"I don't think it'll be easy, but I'll try," Cheryl said slowly.

"Good. And from now on, you've got to be honest with me." Nancy put her hands on Cheryl's shoulders and looked her straight in the eye. "Otherwise, we're never going to get to the bottom of this," she concluded.

After seeing Cheryl to her car, Nancy stood on the curb and thought for a moment. If Chris Gleason was doing his own investigating, his sister might very well know something about it. There was no guarantee that Kate would tell her anything, but Nancy had to talk to her.

Within a few minutes of checking the Gleasons' address in a phone book, Nancy was pulling up in front of a nondescript house in a small town just outside of River Heights.

She rang the doorbell. Kate Gleason came to the door wearing jeans and a sweatshirt. When she saw Nancy, she didn't look happy.

Nancy sighed. She was beginning to get tired of Kate Gleason's attitude, but she had to try to work around it somehow.

"I'm sorry to bother you," she said politely. "But I have to ask you a few questions about your brother."

"Well, you can't come in," Kate said, flipping her hair behind her ears. "My mother is still upset about my dad, and she doesn't want visitors. What do you want to know?" she asked, stepping onto the porch and closing the door.

"Why didn't either of you tell me that Chris was dating Cheryl Pomeroy?" Nancy asked.

In the yellow porch light Nancy watched Kate's eyes narrow. "I don't see what that has to do with anything. My brother can go out with whomever he wants," she challenged.

"Of course he can," Nancy admitted calmly. "But when the person he's dating also happens to have given important evidence to his father, I think it's relevant, don't you?" she asked.

"Look, Nancy. I don't know what you're talking about. Chris and Cheryl have been going together since their senior year in high school. What they do is their business—"

Kate stopped short. The significance of what Nancy had told her must have sunk in. "What do you mean, Cheryl gave my father important evidence?" she asked.

"She told me she did." Briefly, Nancy told Kate about her visit to Mobley and Myerson and what had happened since then.

"So," she concluded, "there seems to be a

lot your brother's not telling you or anyone else."

Kate thought for a moment. "I don't get it. What you're telling me just isn't like Chris. He's been a little aloof lately, but I thought it was because of what happened to our dad."

"It may be," Nancy said. "But I told Cheryl that as far as I'm concerned, Chris's actions seem just the least bit dishonest, not to mention suspicious." Nancy tried to be as gentle as she could with what could appear to be an accusation.

Her tactic didn't work. Kate bristled. "If you came here to ask me to spy on my brother, you can forget it. As far as I'm concerned he's doing what he can to find out what my father knew before he died. Nothing more and nothing less."

"Then why isn't he letting you in on it?" Nancy challenged.

Kate paused. "I don't know," she said finally. Then she changed the subject. "Hey, I thought you were on our side."

"I'm trying to be," Nancy said. There didn't seem to be any way to convince the girl.

"Sure, by coming here with accusations. As far as I can tell, you haven't found out what really happened to my father," she snapped.

"You two aren't really helping me," Nancy said, exasperated.

"Right," Kate said. "I should try to help you

get my brother into trouble. Why don't you just leave us alone now? We'll manage just fine without you, Nancy Drew." With that, Kate stepped back inside and slammed the door shut.

Great, Nancy thought as she got back in her car. The Gleason kids are my only lead and now they think I want to get them into trouble.

Nancy was driving home, thinking about all the dead ends she had run into, when she decided to go back over the most important clue of all—the date book she'd found at Gleason's apartment. The only lead she really had was sitting at home in her desk drawer, and she hadn't looked at it since the first day.

Nancy rushed home. The date book wasn't going to disappear, but she was in a hurry to study it again.

She was letting herself in the front door when Carson appeared in the hallway.

"Nancy, I've been thinking—" he began.

"Dad, I'm really tired. Can it wait until morning?" Nancy faked a yawn. Her mind was already poring over the pages of Gleason's date book. Besides, she didn't want to have to get into a discussion with her father about what she had been doing at Edward Vaughn's office or at Mobley and Myerson.

"I want to talk to you a minute, please." Carson put out his hand to stop her. "After you left, reporters started calling," he said.

Nancy let out a gasp. "It's okay," Carson went on. "I'm fine."

"What specifically did they want to know?" Nancy asked, sitting down on a step leading upstairs.

"It seems that all of River Heights is buzzing with the news that I may have suppressed evidence the DA subpoenaed in the Allard trial," Carson said with a sigh.

"So now the DA thinks you tried to frame Gleason by withholding evidence?"

Carson nodded. "That's right. But I didn't!"

Nancy had never seen her father so worked up. "I know you didn't, Dad," she said. She stood up and wrapped her arms around him, hardly able to believe this was happening to them.

Carson hugged her back, then pulled away. He let out a deep breath. "You're right, Nancy. We can't stand by and let this go on. I'll take all the help I can get."

Now, there's the father I know and love, Nancy thought. She felt tears welling up in her eyes. "What's the first step?" she asked.

"Follow me," Carson said. He went into the living room, Nancy following him.

Carson handed her a thick manila file folder, bursting with documents. "What's this?" she asked, taking it from her father.

"My records from the trial," he explained. "I dragged them out and started going through them. And you'll never believe what I found," he said excitedly.

Nancy gave her father a bright look. "Don't keep me in suspense, Dad."

Carson smiled. "You're never going to believe this," he said. "Do you remember that the embezzled money disappeared from a bank account the day before the indictments were handed down?"

Nancy nodded.

"But this is what I hadn't remembered—the money had supposedly been transferred to an account at the River Heights Bank and Trust."

"Do you realize what you're saying?" Nancy asked. "That's the same bank that Dennis Allard works at now!"

"That's right, kiddo. One and the same."

Chapter

Eleven

NANCY STARED unblinking at her father. "You are thinking the same thing I'm thinking, aren't you?" she asked slowly. "That this isn't just some strange coincidence."

"Well," he said, "I don't think we can jump to conclusions."

Nancy was about to interrupt, until Carson went on, obviously excited at the discovery. "But it is a little strange that the same man who was involved in the embezzlement case should end up working in the bank where the embezzled money had been transferred to and disappeared from."

"And this same man claims not to know anything about it."

Carson pulled a piece of paper from the folder. "Look at this," he said, pointing. "The day before the indictments came down, all the money that had been transferred there from the clients' overpayments was withdrawn. In cash. Robert Gleason signed the check."

"But Gleason insisted he didn't know anything about the money," Nancy said, leafing through the pages.

"I know. Nancy, there's too much that's wrong here."

"You don't know the half of it," Nancy said. She started pacing the room. Everything in the case seemed to be breaking at once.

"I've come to the conclusion that Chris Gleason knows something about where the money is. Or is trying his hardest to find it," she told her father.

"So you weren't with George just now, were you?" Carson asked, a grin spreading over his face. "Come on, Nancy. I'm your father, I can tell when something's up."

Nancy was so relieved her father was finally on her side that the whole story spilled out of her.

"Dad, I followed Cheryl Pomeroy," she told him. "You're never going to believe this, but the reason she gave Gleason the file in the first place was because she's going with Chris Gleason. She also told me that Chris has been to see Dennis Allard. It looks like he's obsessed with the money that was never found."

Carson rubbed his chin thoughtfully. "So you think his main reason for getting you to investigate his father's death is to lead him to the money?"

Nancy nodded.

"I'm going to change my mind again. I think it's time I called the district attorney and told him my side of the story, including all of this about the Gleasons," Carson said firmly. "And tomorrow I'm going to do just that."

"But, Dad—" Nancy began.

"No buts," Carson said. He came over to where she was standing by the fireplace and put a hand on her shoulder. "You've done more than enough for now. You are officially off the case again. I know you're trying to help me, but you're in over your head. I have to think of you. Now you really should get to bed. It's late."

Nancy went upstairs. She knew her father was right. He had to call the DA, to try to clear his name if nothing else.

But that didn't mean she wasn't going to continue to get to the bottom of Chris Gleason's motives. If he *was* using her, there was no way she was going to let him get away with it.

Nancy was in bed before she remembered Gleason's date book.

I'm really losing my touch, she said to herself. She got up, opened her desk drawer, and took out the small notebook.

Going page by page backward from the day Gleason died, Nancy pored over the notebook once more. She saw that Gleason had had appointments with Cheryl Pomeroy, Peter Nicodemus, Dennis Allard—nothing she didn't already know. There had to be something important in the book if Gleason had bothered to hide it.

After nearly an hour of trying to find any clue in the notebook, Nancy turned off her light. She decided that the next day she was going to get some answers from the two people who had to know more than they were telling: Chris Gleason and Dennis Allard.

"I was just about to call you," Bess told Nancy on the phone the next morning. "How's your dad?"

Nancy briefly explained what had happened the night before. "Are you ready for action?" she asked her friend.

"You bet!" Bess answered. "Anything."

Nancy gave Kate Gleason's address to Bess. "Get over there as fast as you can and watch her. If she leaves, follow her. I have a feeling she's up to something and I want to know what it is. Then meet me and George for lunch at Bonne Cuisine in the mall at twelve-thirty."

"Gotcha," Bess said, hanging up.

Next Nancy called George, who was also more than happy to help her out.

"Cheryl Pomeroy, watch out," she said, after Nancy had explained what she wanted George to do. "Because wherever you go, I'll be there," she said, laughing.

"Thanks, George. And let's meet for lunch at Bonne Cuisine at twelve-thirty to talk about what you found out." Nancy hung up the phone and left the house.

After the short drive downtown in her rented car, Nancy pulled up in front of River Heights Bank and Trust. She wanted to find out if there was any way to trace the money. Nancy also had to determine whether or not there was any reason to suspect Dennis Allard.

A few minutes later she was standing outside Dennis Allard's office.

"Mr. Allard will be with you in a minute," a young secretary told her, pointing to a chair. "Have a seat." Then the girl walked away on stiletto heels. I've seen enough secretaries and receptionists on this case to last me a lifetime, Nancy thought.

Nancy walked around the small outer office. From the lone voice inside Allard's office,

Nancy assumed he was on the phone. She moved closer to his door, noticing it was slightly ajar.

"Don't worry," she heard him saying. "Everything's under control. Yes. I said don't worry." Then Nancy saw him catch her eye. "I'll talk to you later," he said, quickly finishing his conversation.

Nancy covered herself by knocking softly on the door. "Can I come in?" she asked.

"Of course," Allard said with a smile. "Just taking care of some business. What can I do for you today? Still thinking about the Gleason case?" he asked.

"Actually, yes," Nancy answered. "I've been thinking about the missing money. Last night my father told me that the embezzled money had been stashed in the bank."

"I seem to remember that was the case," Allard said, rubbing his chin. "But from what I recall, the money disappeared from here, and none of it was ever recovered."

"I was hoping you could help me find it, though." It was a long shot, Nancy knew. Banks had all sorts of laws against anyone looking at their records.

Allard seemed to read her mind. "You realize I can't really allow you to see those records," he said.

"I know it would be asking a lot," Nancy

said. "But this is the last time I'll ask for your help." She watched Allard's face for some kind of reaction, but his features remained a blank.

"I'll hold you to it," he said, smiling. "It's a little unorthodox, but I still feel as if I owe Carson Drew a favor. Come with me."

As Allard took Nancy down to the bank's record room, Nancy thought about how helpful he was being. If he was guilty, Allard had everything to lose by cooperating with her. Instead, he was even bending the law a bit to allow her to look at the records. That wasn't the act of a guilty man, she thought.

In the records room, Nancy saw stacks of computer printouts; several people were seated at terminals and microfiche readers working on bank statements.

"Alan here can help you," Allard said, introducing her to a tall young man with thick blond hair and preppy round glasses. "Explain to him what you're looking for and maybe, between the two of you, you'll find it."

Nancy thanked Allard and started telling Alan about Gleason's bank account.

"Let's see," Alan said. His fingers quickly tapped out Gleason's name. "Eight years ago, you say. Hmmm. Here it is." With a few keystrokes, Alan had pulled up a record of the account.

"Withdrawal. Closed out the account.

Whew! That's a lot of money to take out all at once."

"Can you see if there's a record of a deposit around the same day for the same amount?" Nancy asked. "I'm trying to find out if the money appeared in some other account."

"Good thought," Alan said. *Tap, tap.* "Nope. Nothing. No large deposits into either a checking or a savings account."

"Are you sure?" Nancy felt her disappointment rising.

"Look, I'm a pro. If I can't find it, no one can. That's what I told the other guy who was here a few days ago asking the same thing. What is it with this account, anyway? You're not from the IRS, are you?" Alan looked at Nancy over his glasses.

"Me? No." Nancy barely even heard the question. "What's that you said about 'the other guy'?"

"Mr. Allard brought a kid down here several days ago and told me to help him out the same way." Alan leaned back in his chair. "I don't know what you people are doing, but personally, I have better things to do with my time."

There was only one other person who would be so interested in the account, Nancy realized. "Sorry," Nancy distractedly told Alan. "I'll let you get back to work." She headed for the door.

"That kid, was he about six feet tall with

wavy brown hair and green eyes?" she turned to ask.

"Yep," Alan said. "Is he a friend of yours?"

"Sort of," Nancy said, as she left.

She and Chris Gleason had a lot to talk about and it couldn't wait another minute.

Nancy remembered that Cheryl had said Chris worked at a foreign-car shop in River Heights. At the second one she checked Nancy spotted a familiar figure working under a Porsche up on the lift.

"Chris," she said, coming up to him. "I think you have some explaining to do."

Chris turned around. "Oh, it's you. Look, I'm busy. Can it wait?"

"No, it can't," she said firmly. Chris looked at her with a puzzled expression.

Nancy went on. "If you want me to help you find out who killed your father—if he really was killed—why are you doing your own investigating? What's going on?"

"Look, Nancy, I can't talk now. Maybe later." Chris went back to work under the car.

Nancy looked around and saw that aside from the car Chris was working on, things seemed to be slow at the garage. She felt herself getting angry.

"Can't you take a break?" she asked.

"I told you—" Chris began. Nancy saw him look up. "That's strange—"

"What?" she asked.

Then Nancy saw what had caught his attention. With quick jerks, the lift holding up the Porsche was losing height. The car was rapidly lurching toward the ground.

And they were standing right beneath it!

Chapter

Twelve

GET OUT OF THE WAY!"

Chris pushed Nancy to the ground. At that moment the car crashed all the way to the garage floor. Two of its hubcaps hurtled off, spun in the air for a moment, and settled down in a metallic whir.

"What—" Chris rolled over Nancy and picked himself up.

Nancy sat up, dazed and shaking. She watched as Chris went over to inspect the damage to the car.

Slowly Nancy got up off the garage floor, brushing off her jeans. On wobbly legs, she went over to the air compressor that kept the pneumatic lift up. With a shock, she saw the air hose connecting the compressor to the lift had a deep slash mark in it.

"Chris, take a look at this." Nancy pointed the gash out to him when he came over. "It looks like someone wanted that lift to fall on you," she said slowly.

Chris squinted his eyes and bent down to look more carefully at the hose. After he saw the torn hose, he looked up at Nancy, wide-eyed.

"I think you're right," he said. "The compressor had only been on for a few minutes, so I had no way of knowing the lift wasn't getting enough air. And with this running"—he pointed to the pneumatic drill lying beside the Porsche—"it's impossible to hear a thing."

"Did you see anyone around here this morning?" Nancy asked him.

"No one," Chris said, shaking his head. "But it had to have happened while the garage was open, because we lock up at night." Chris ran his hands through his hair and looked again at the compressor.

Nancy took a deep breath. "Maybe you can see now why I need to talk to you. This"—she pointed to the Porsche—"is pretty serious. Someone obviously is sending you a warning."

"You may be right," Chris agreed.

"So when can we all get together to talk?"

Nancy asked. "You, your sister, Cheryl, and me?"

"Unfortunately, I'm not free until tomorrow," Chris said. "I'm the only one here today." Nancy sighed. "I wish I could do it sooner, but I can't," he added weakly.

"Then lunch tomorrow," Nancy said firmly. "Let's meet in the mall at Bonne Cuisine. And I'd suggest you lay low until then."

As Nancy drove away, she wondered who would threaten Chris Gleason and why he still seemed to be holding back. She decided to ask Bess and George what they thought over lunch.

"It was the funniest thing," Bess said after the three girls had been served. "I followed Kate, and who should I meet up with but George."

"I saw Bess's car outside the health club and asked her what she was doing there," George continued. "We had a good laugh when we realized we were both there following someone."

"So Kate and Cheryl met and worked out together. What else?" Nancy asked.

"Nothing happened with Cheryl." George shook her head. "Cheryl went off to work—very late."

"And Kate did some shopping," Bess added. "What's new on your front?"

Nancy waited for the waitress to put their plates down before she told her friends about what had happened at the garage.

"Wow. Someone is playing for keeps," Bess said, taking a bite of her salad. "And you could have been killed, too."

Nancy nodded, staring into space.

George brought her back with a jolt. "Nancy, what's on your mind?" she asked.

Nancy shook her head slowly. "I just can't figure out what to make of this case," she said. "It looks like Chris has his eye on the money, but I don't think he's found it."

"Meanwhile, neither of the Gleasons is helping you very much," George said.

"That's true," Nancy agreed.

"But they asked you to get involved in the first place," Bess pointed out.

"It's pretty strange," George admitted. "Hey, I've got an idea. Why don't we all meet tomorrow, and Bess and I will keep our eyes on them while you try to get at the truth?"

"Great idea, George," Nancy said. "I've already planned on doing just that. Lunch tomorrow. Here." After wolfing down the rest of her sandwich, Nancy looked at her watch. "I'd better be going. I want to call my dad and find out what happened with the DA. Meet you two outside?"

Nancy left George and Bess to pay the check.

She found a phone booth to call her father, and after a minute he came on the line.

"I told him everything, Nancy," Carson said. "And he wants to meet with you, as soon as possible, to hear everything you know."

"Okay, Dad," Nancy said with a sigh. "I'll head over there now with Bess and George."

As she hung up, Nancy hoped the DA wasn't going to tell her to quit her investigation. She felt too involved now to want to let someone else take over.

Nancy walked back to the restaurant. "We've got an appointment with the DA," she told Bess and George, who were standing outside.

"We?" Bess asked.

"You got it," Nancy answered. "And I'd hate to keep him waiting, so let's go!"

"Nancy, could you please explain all this?" Bess said as they wandered through the city office building.

"My father insisted I go to the district attorney to tell him everything I know," Nancy explained. "I want the two of you along because I want to ask him a favor, and if he agrees, I'm going to need your help. Here we are," she said, pushing open a door with District Attorney stenciled in big black letters.

Inside, the office was filled with ancient

desks and filing cabinets piled high with papers, folders, and stacks of what looked like legal documents. And, Nancy noticed as she just stifled a sneeze, the whole place was covered in dust.

Bess, George, and Nancy introduced themselves and waited while the receptionist buzzed the district attorney on the intercom.

"Nancy Drew to see you? Right," she said, hanging up the phone. "Go ahead. First and only door in that corridor to your right."

The three friends made their way around several desks crowded together in the middle of the room. Nancy knocked softly on the door. A thin, balding man only slightly taller than she opened it.

"Joseph Levine," he said, offering his hand.

"Nancy Drew," she said. "And these are my friends, Bess Marvin and George Fayne."

"Nice to meet you," Levine said. "Come on in. Sorry about the mess, but somehow cleaning up never makes it to the top of my list of things to do." He laughed.

After Levine cleared papers off three chairs, the girls sat down.

"Now that we're all comfortable," Levine said, "why don't you tell me why you're here? Mr. Drew's explained a little bit, but I'd like to hear it straight from the detective's mouth, as it were." Levine laughed again.

Nancy smiled. Then she took a deep breath

and launched into a description of what had happened over the past few days.

"As you can see," she concluded, "there are a lot of loose ends. Did Gleason really commit suicide? What's the missing evidence? Where's the money, and do the Gleason kids care more about that than their father?"

"And," the DA added, "was Robert Gleason guilty in the first place?"

"Exactly," Nancy said.

Bess and George had been silent while Nancy told the story. Now George let out a half sigh, half whistle.

"To hear you tell it that way, Nancy, I just realized how messy this case really is," she said.

"Not really," the DA said. "It seems to me that the first thing we have to do is find out whether or not Gleason killed himself. I'll take care of that side of the investigation." Joe Levine got up from behind his desk, came around in front of Nancy and sat on his desk. He looked her straight in the eye.

"Your father said he didn't want you to be involved in this anymore. You know that, don't you?" he asked.

Nancy swallowed and looked down at her feet. "I know. But it's really tough when your own father's career could be on the line," she said.

"I agree." Levine paused. "I'm required to

investigate all the sides of the law. You know there may be proof that your father suppressed evidence eight years ago?"

Nancy nodded. Bess and George were silent.

"That story was never supposed to be leaked. It's an ongoing investigation, and Carson Drew has yet to be charged." He shook his head. "But it happened. Meanwhile, I don't have any authority to take you off the case."

The three friends exchanged a look. "That's good news," Nancy said, relieved.

"I do have some advice for you, though," Levine said firmly. "No more funny business. Anything you learn, you tell me. It'll only help your father," he pointed out.

Nancy looked down and bit on her lower lip. She was thinking about Gleason's notebook back home in her room. "Then I guess I should tell you. I took something from Robert Gleason's apartment."

"What?" Bess and George said in unison.

She explained to Levine and her friends about the notebook. When she was finished, Levine said simply, with no room for argument, "You'd better return it first thing tomorrow."

Nancy nodded. "I promise," she said. "I have one more favor to ask: Would it be all right if my friends and I did a little research in the trial archives?"

Bess and George looked surprised. Joe Levine rested his chin between his index finger and the palm of his hand, trying to figure out what Nancy had in mind.

"Sure," he said eventually. "But what do you hope to find?"

"Remember that evidence Cheryl Pomeroy found?" Nancy asked. Levine nodded. "Well," she went on, "it's been bothering me. I just can't figure out what it might be."

"And you want to go through the old trial records to see if there isn't something missing?" Levine concluded.

"Right," Nancy said. "I doubt anything will turn up, but it's the only way I can think of to figure out why Gleason got so excited about the evidence. And why someone might have killed him for it."

"If he was killed," Levine said, staring hard at Nancy. "That remains to be proven."

Two hours later Nancy, Bess, and George had plowed through hundreds of pages of transcripts from the trial and several notebooks full of descriptions of exhibits that had been introduced.

"I don't think I can take much more of this," Bess said. "This is so boring. On television trials always seem so glamorous. Who would ever have thought that they were mostly a lot of paperwork."

"You said it," George agreed, rubbing her

eyes. "I'm still not sure what we're looking for here, Nancy."

"I wasn't sure, either, George," Nancy said. "But I think I've found something that may be important. Read this." She handed George a page of the trial transcript.

George's eyes quickly scanned the page. "It looks to me like more of the same. Gleason insisting he's innocent, that he's been framed. But without any proof, what good is it?"

"George, you just said the magic word: proof," Nancy said excitedly. "Gleason told Cheryl that the file she gave him would prove that he was innocent. So what kind of proof would he need? Proof that he didn't do the embezzling, that the program the prosecution accused him of writing he hadn't written."

"Take a look." She pointed to a spot in the trial transcript.

Bess and George quickly scanned the page. "From what I can tell, Gleason claimed there was a real program written for a set of phony books, kept by the 'real' embezzler," George said.

"And that program they say he wrote was part of an elaborate frame," Nancy concluded.

"Hold on, Nancy," Bess said. "I'm not sure I follow. What you're saying is that there were two programs written with phony books: one that was used only to frame Gleason, and one that was really used by the real embezzler?"

"I know it sounds crazy," Nancy admitted. "But it's the only answer."

"Nancy," Bess squeaked. "Do you realize what that means?"

"That Gleason was innocent," Nancy finished for her. "And Dennis Allard was guilty after all."

Chapter

Thirteen

BUT MR. ALLARD seemed like such a nice man," Bess said mournfully. "And now it looks like he not only was guilty, but that he was also the one trying to get your father into serious trouble."

Nancy wasn't really listening to her friend. Her mind was on Dennis Allard. Then something Bess said brought her back to the present. "Bess, what did you just say?"

"That he could be the one trying to get your father into trouble," Bess repeated.

"That's ridiculous," George said. "Why would he want to bring it all up again? He got off scot-free."

"It's not so strange an idea, really," Nancy said, thinking. "What if he knew that Gleason was on to him? The logical thing would be for him to throw suspicion onto someone else."

"But how would he know that?" George asked.

"I'm not sure," Nancy said. "But I'm going to find out."

Nancy, Bess, and George were back at Bonne Cuisine the next day, waiting for Cheryl Pomeroy and Chris and Kate Gleason to show up. Nancy was explaining her plan.

"Here they are now," she said as the door opened and the Gleasons and Cheryl Pomeroy walked into the restaurant.

"Well, we're all here," Kate said glumly. The three sat down. "Are you going to explain what this is all about?"

Chris sat there rapping his fingers on the table. Cheryl reached over and put her hand over his. Nancy looked at Kate.

"I thought you'd like to know that I'm this close"—she put her thumb and forefinger close together—"to solving the case."

"That's great!" Kate blurted out. "I can't believe it. Do you know who killed my father?"

Nancy shook her head. "That I still don't know. But the district attorney is working on it

117

and he's going to let me know as soon as there's some kind of proof."

"It looks to me like you're missing all kinds of proof," Chris challenged. "Don't you think you're jumping the gun? How can you pretend to be close to solving the case if you don't even have a suspect?" He jutted out his chin and squinted his eyes. "Some detective," he muttered to himself.

"Take it easy, Chris," Cheryl said quietly.

"Actually, I think I've done pretty well, considering," Nancy answered. "For example, I know you went to see Dennis Allard." Nancy watched as Chris sank a little in his chair. "And," she continued, "I think I found what you were looking for that day in your father's apartment."

With that, Nancy pulled her prop from her purse. Earlier, she'd taken Gleason's notebook to the DA, but beforehand she'd copied the pages into an identical notebook. She threw it on the table in front of Chris.

Chris reached for it, but Nancy put her hands over the notebook before he could pick it up.

"How did you find that?" Chris asked, pulling his hand back.

Bess and George looked at each other while Cheryl tried to put her arm around Chris. He pulled away. "What makes you think you can just steal my father's personal property?"

"That's not as important as why, if you really want me to solve this case, you're working on your own and won't tell me anything," Nancy answered. She wasn't going to let him get the best of her this time.

Chris sighed. "All right," he said. "I did go to see Allard. But there's a good reason why I did. I thought the evidence might have something to do with the missing money—which is why I went to see Allard."

"But how did you know about the notebook?" George asked.

"For as long as I've known my father, he's kept a date book in an ordinary notebook like that," he explained. "It was one of his idiosyncrasies."

Nancy leaned on the table and gave Chris a long, hard look. "I agree with you. There's probably a clue here about where your father hid the evidence Cheryl gave him, but I couldn't find it."

"But if you give it to Chris," Bess pointed out, "there's a chance he might find something you missed."

"I might. I know my father's habits pretty well, and I'd recognize something that was out of the ordinary," Chris said.

"What makes you want to trust us now?" Cheryl asked.

Nancy scanned the Gleasons' faces. It was a good question. She waited and could see that Kate was holding her breath expectantly.

"I don't know," Nancy said finally. "But I guess I have no choice. There's one thing I'm still worried about, though."

"What's that?" Kate asked anxiously.

"The money. I want to know for certain it's not the money you're after," Nancy said.

"I know it probably looks that way," Kate began.

"You've got to believe me when I say I'm only interested in clearing my father's name," Chris said earnestly. "And finding out who killed him."

Nancy glanced at Bess and George. So far the Gleasons hadn't been the most trustworthy brother-and-sister team.

George gave her an encouraging nod. "I believe them, Nancy," Bess said.

She had to trust her friends' judgment. "Take the notebook," Nancy said. "And do whatever you can to find a clue about where the evidence might be. Before we can clear your father we have to find the evidence or the money or both. It's the only proof we've got."

Kate got up to leave with her brother and his girlfriend.

"Thank you, Nancy," she said, giving her a wan smile. "I know we haven't given you anything but trouble, and I'm sorry. I really didn't trust you until you gave us the notebook just now. From now on we're going to work as a team. I promise."

"Scout's honor," Chris said, holding up three fingers. "We'll be on our best behavior from now on." He put his arm around Cheryl, who smiled for the first time since they had all sat down.

Nancy watched as the three walked away.

"You did the right thing, Nan," George said. "Now, where do we go from here?"

"I want to stake out Dennis Allard," Nancy said. "I need to try to find out exactly what he's up to."

"Should we come along? You could probably use our help," George said. Bess nodded in agreement.

"I don't think so, guys," Nancy said, getting up. "I'd better do it alone—it'll arouse less suspicion. But stay close by. I'm sure I'll need your help again soon."

The three parted ways in the parking lot. As Nancy got into her rented car, she could tell that Bess and George looked worried.

"Be careful, Nan," Bess said.

George turned to her cousin. "She'll be fine. Nancy's done this before."

"Thanks for the vote of confidence," Nancy said, starting her car. "I'll let you know what happens."

Nancy roared off in the direction of Allard's bank. She checked her watch. It was only two o'clock. If she had to wait, she would.

Two hours later Nancy was still sitting in front of River Heights Bank and Trust when she finally spotted Dennis Allard coming out of the building.

I'm lucky he keeps bankers' hours, Nancy thought. She started her car to be ready to follow Allard at a safe distance.

Nancy didn't know what she'd find out by tailing Dennis Allard. But after an hour of following him, all she knew was where he got his hair cut and which dry cleaner he used.

This is getting me nowhere fast, she thought. If something doesn't happen soon, I'm going home.

Then Allard led her to a run-down section of small businesses, where he stopped his car and got out. Nancy watched as he let himself into a building painted a garish shade of green.

After waiting a few minutes Nancy went inside also. The building was three stories high and a rickety wooden staircase led to the upper stories. She had no way of telling which floor Allard had stopped on, but on the wall across from the staircase was an old building directory.

Nancy scanned the directory for Allard's name or any other name she might recognize. Nothing. She took out her notepad and quickly wrote down the names of all six companies, leaving out one that was named Lee's Nails because it was obviously a manicure shop.

She was about to leave the building when she heard footsteps on the second floor landing. Nancy looked up through the railing and saw a figure coming down the stairs. Dennis Allard!

Quickly, Nancy made her way down the short corridor that ran beside the staircase.

At the end of the corridor she thought she had seen a window that she could use for a possible escape. The footsteps were getting closer.

Nancy quietly planted herself against the wall, under the staircase, hoping that Allard hadn't seen her. She was looking toward the window and planning her escape when she felt a strong hand on her shoulder.

Nancy turned around. It was Dennis Allard, his face red with fury.

Chapter

Fourteen

"MR. ALLARD," Nancy said, trying not to stammer. "What a coincidence. It's so funny we should run into each other here."

"It is, isn't it?" Allard asked, giving Nancy a strange look.

I'd better come up with an excuse fast, Nancy thought.

"My favorite manicurist of all time has her shop here. She used to be closer to my house, but then she moved and I couldn't find anyone else who had such a gentle touch." Nancy rattled off her story. Maybe Allard would buy the flighty teenager routine.

"She must be good if you came such a long

way," Allard remarked, looking closely at Nancy.

"Well, I'd better be getting home. I'm sure my dad's wondering where I am. You know how fathers can be." Nancy kept up the patter while she made her way out of the building. Allard stayed by her side until she had gotten in her car and started the engine.

"How's the investigation going?" Allard asked before Nancy could drive away.

"You know," Nancy said, "it's the strangest thing, but now the police think Robert Gleason may have been murdered." She searched Allard's face for a reaction, but he didn't blink an eye.

"That is bizarre," he said. "But I'm sure they know what they're doing."

"There are so many weird things about this case," she concluded, shaking her head. "Well, gotta go. See you later."

Nancy watched in her rearview mirror as Allard waited for her to drive off. It's only a matter of time, she thought, before Dennis Allard starts wondering what I'm up to. If he hasn't already.

On her way home Nancy decided to stop at the River Heights Library. She didn't want to waste any time in finding out what Allard was doing in that green building. She decided to do a little research on the companies she had written down before Allard discovered her.

When Nancy got to the library, she spied her favorite librarian, Ed Nesky, working at the circulation desk.

"Ed," she said, going up to him. "I need your help."

Ed gave Nancy a crooked smile. He was always happy to help her out with research on cases. "What's up?" he asked, looking at her with his hazel eyes.

"If I have the name of a company, is there any way to find out who runs it?" Nancy asked.

"No problem. Give me a minute and I'll show you where to look." Nancy waited while Ed went over to his supervisor and explained that he had to leave the desk for a few minutes.

"Follow me," he said, pulling Nancy by the elbow. "This is where you should look." He pointed out a series of tall, thick volumes. There must have been nearly thirty in all.

"Who Owns What," Nancy said, reading the spines. "Are you kidding?" She laughed and then smiled at Ed.

"Nope. It's for real. Funny title, right?" Ed grinned and ran his hands through his straight hair. "Companies are listed alphabetically, with their owners or directors following. Sometimes you'll have one company owned by another, though, so you might have to check three or four places before you find out who really owns it."

"Thanks, Ed," Nancy said, raising her eyebrows. "This isn't going to be as easy as I thought."

"Have fun," Ed said, chuckling as he walked away.

One by one, Nancy went through the list of the six companies she had written down. Although she wanted to, she didn't rule out Lee's Nails. You never know, she told herself.

After half an hour Nancy hadn't found out anything and she was down to just two companies: Convex Corporation and the Alladin Group.

"Find anything yet?" Ed was leaning over her shoulder as Nancy looked up the Alladin Group.

"Nothing yet," she said.

"Want some help?"

"I'd love it. This is getting a little tedious, but I'm down to just two. Can you check out Convex Corporation for me?" she asked.

"Sure." Ed went over and pulled the volume with *C* in it from the shelf while Nancy went back to researching the Alladin Group. Nothing related to Dennis Allard there, even though she had hoped there would be. The name sounded a lot like his.

Ed sat down next to her then. "I don't know if this means anything to you," he said, "but Convex Corporation has two owners."

"What are their names?" Nancy asked.

"See for yourself," Ed said, pushing the volume across the table to her.

Nancy ran her fingers down the page, coming to Convex Corporation. "'Owned by,'" she read, then stopped. "I can't believe it!" she practically shouted. "'Dennis Allard and Peter Nicodemus'!" She finally had the connection she'd been looking for.

Nancy thanked Ed and headed out of the library. She couldn't believe her luck.

Nicodemus had worked at the firm when the embezzling took place. Now he and Allard were in business together. That can't be a coincidence, she thought. What if Nicodemus had been involved with Allard in the embezzlement?

There was one way to find out, she realized, and she headed quickly in the direction of Mobley and Myerson.

As she drove to Nicodemus's building, Nancy tried to devise a plan for getting into the building and offices. It wouldn't be easy, and there was a good chance that some of the lawyers might be working late.

Along the way, she devised her plan. With all the secretaries she'd seen on this case, she knew she could pose as one of them.

Getting past the security guard in the lobby was easier than she thought it would be. She told him she was a temporary secretary and that she had left her purse in the office. He let her by without even making her sign the building register.

At first Nancy was going to take the elevator to Nicodemus's floor. Then she realized it would be easier to get into the offices if she went to the floor below Nicodemus's and took the internal stairs.

When the elevator doors opened on the fourteenth floor, Nancy saw her opportunity. One of the cleaning crews had left an oversize trash can on wheels outside the bank of elevators.

Nancy put on a pair of rubber gloves she found hanging over the trash can and wheeled it through the firm's glass doors. If anyone asked her what she was doing there, she'd answer that she was a new member of the cleaning crew.

After a few wrong turns, Nancy found the firm's internal stairs and dragged the garbage can up the short flight. She made her way in the direction of Nicodemus's office.

Most of the lights were out in this part of the firm. Nancy heard a few voices at the end of the hallway, but realized they were coming from the opposite direction of Nicodemus's office.

Quickly Nancy pushed the garbage can down the hall and stopped outside Nicodemus's office. She tried the knob. The door was unlocked. Slowly she inched the door open, her heart pounding. Nicodemus wasn't inside.

All the lights were on, but Nicodemus wasn't there. Nancy hurried over to his desk. There, she saw an employee file and several pink message slips laid out on the top of it. Nancy quickly opened the file. It belonged to Cheryl Pomeroy. Maybe Nicodemus suspects something's up with her, Nancy thought.

Then Nancy picked up one of the message slips. It was a reminder that Dennis Allard had called. The time on the slip was right after Allard had caught Nancy in his building!

She scanned Nicodemus's bookshelves and ran her eyes over his desk. Then she started searching through the other papers on his desk.

Before Nancy could start on anything, she heard voices in the hallway. She stood perfectly still and listened. They were moving closer and closer toward Nicodemus's office.

Nancy held her breath. She was about to be caught red-handed in Peter Nicodemus's office!

Chapter

Fifteen

A WAVE OF FEAR passed over her. There wasn't going to be an easy explanation for why she was in Peter Nicodemus's office. If it were Nicodemus himself who was heading her way, she was in even worse trouble.

After giving the office a wistful glance—she'd have given anything for the opportunity to really search the place—Nancy slipped out the door.

At one end of the long hallway, Nancy saw two figures deep in conversation. Most of the hall lights were off, so Nancy was in shadow too. Without stopping to see whether or not it was Nicodemus at the end of the hall, Nancy took off in the opposite direction.

She crossed the hallway and dashed around a corner. She had nearly made her way to the small flight of stairs that would take her back down to safety when she heard a voice call out.

"Hold it right there!" a man shouted. "Stop!"

Nancy desperately looked around for an escape. Then she spied her only chance. Ten feet ahead of her there was a fire door with the word Exit in red lettering.

Quickly Nancy ran to the door and pushed it open. A clamorous din of alarms greeted her as she found herself in a half-lit stairwell.

Nancy took a second for her eyes to adjust to the darkness. Then she flew down the steps, taking them three at a time, sliding her hand down the railing for balance.

One flight down, Nancy heard footsteps on the stairs behind her. She forced herself not to turn around and look but to continue her flying leaps instead.

Then Nancy heard the loud, unmistakable blast of a shot echoing over and over in the stairwell. The bullet ricocheted off the cement wall only inches from her.

She had no choice. Almost without thinking, Nancy leapt over the railing. She banged her knee badly but hardly felt the blow.

After landing with a bone-jarring crash one

flight down, Nancy ducked. Another shot sent shards of cement flying above her head.

Unless she could find some way to disarm her pursuer, Nancy knew she was trapped. She jumped the railing again down still another flight, and, before getting up, took a second to think. In a flash, she thought of one slim possibility. It might work.

She pounded her feet, making loud running sounds. Then she threw herself to the ground in the shadow of the staircase and waited breathlessly.

In a few seconds Nancy spied Peter Nicodemus charging down the stairs, taking them two at a time. She leaned farther into the shadows, making herself as small as possible until just the right moment. Then, when he was within striking distance, she put out her leg and sent him flying.

Nicodemus stumbled to his knees and looked at Nancy for a moment before losing his balance and sailing down the flight of stairs. Nancy took off after him and jumped over the last step as Nicodemus landed in a heap at her feet.

Before he had the chance to reach for his gun again, Nancy raised her right arm and brought it down with a resounding crack right between his shoulder blades. The man sank down again, this time unconscious.

Nancy didn't wait for him to wake up. She

took one deep breath and ran as fast as she could down the remaining flights of stairs. If she was lucky, he wouldn't revive until she was well on her way to safety.

"You're lucky to be alive," Kate said as she gave Nancy an ice pack.

They were sitting in Robert Gleason's living room on what passed for a sofa. After her ordeal, Nancy had called Kate and Chris at home, and they'd arranged to meet, along with Cheryl, at Gleason's apartment. It seemed a private place to plan their next move.

"Don't I know it," Nancy said. She put the ice on her knee, which was swelling pretty badly. "But we don't have time to think about it. Nicodemus has probably been in touch with Allard by now and they've already planned their next move."

Chris looked up. He was poring over his father's notebook. "I wish I had some good news," he said. "But I haven't been able to come up with anything concrete."

Kate's eyes grew large with either fear or disappointment, Nancy couldn't tell. But she knew they had to come up with something fast.

"Go over it again," Kate said, wringing her hands. "We've got to find that evidence."

"I've tried. But there's nothing here except what we already know. Appointments with Cheryl and Allard. Errands. Notes."

"What do the notes say?" Nancy asked, hobbling to the table and leaning over Chris's shoulder.

"Lawyer. Drew. Allard. DA. Bank. Vaughn. I'm telling you, there's nothing here except gibberish."

"Wait a minute," Nancy said. "Let me see."

Nancy quickly went back to the day Gleason had an appointment with Allard, then flipped the pages forward one by one.

"Why," she asked, "would your father have gone back to River Heights Bank and Trust the day before he died if he'd already met with Allard? It wouldn't have done him any good. Unless he wanted to try to trace the money as you and I did."

"But," said Chris, "I asked that guy—what's his name? Alan?—if my dad had been there, and he said no."

"You're sure?" Nancy asked.

"Positive."

"Then there had to be some other reason." She closed the pages of the notebook, got up, and began pacing the room, favoring her sore right leg.

"Why else go to a bank? Not to open an account—he didn't have any money. But he's got a note here." She went back to the date book and found the page she was looking for. "It says, 'bring passport.' Why bring a passport to a bank if you're not going to open an account?"

Nancy stood up straight. Then she banged her forehead with the ball of her left hand.

"I can't believe how stupid I've been," she said. "All the time, it's been staring us right in the face."

"What has?" Kate asked. "Don't keep us dangling."

Nancy went over what they knew. "Cheryl gave your father a computer file that contained a set of books that proved he'd been framed by Dennis Allard, right?"

Cheryl nodded. "It looks that way."

"And your father wanted to make sure it was safe until he could give it to the DA," Nancy said excitedly. The pieces were all coming together.

"Slow down," Chris said. "Why didn't he take it straight to Levine? Why wait?" he asked.

Nancy shook her head. "I don't know," she said slowly. "But the day before he died, he went back to River Heights Bank and Trust. And that's where he hid the evidence!"

"What?" Chris practically shouted.

"Your father did what a lot of people do," Nancy concluded. "He hid the evidence in the most obvious place possible. At Allard's bank. In a safe deposit box."

"Of course," Chris said. "The printout

would be small enough to hide in a safe deposit box."

Kate ran to Nancy and flung her arms around Nancy's neck. "Oh, Nancy, thank you," she said, her voice breaking.

"Hold on," Nancy said, pulling Kate's arms from around her. "There's no guarantee it's there. But if it is, we've got to get to it before Allard does. If he hasn't already."

"But Allard couldn't have known where it was, or else he'd have destroyed it by now and he'd have nothing to worry about," Chris said.

"True enough," Nancy said. "But we can't take any chances. I'm going to call the District Attorney."

Nancy went over to the far end of the kitchen and picked up the phone. Then she realized that there was no chance that the DA would still be at the office at this hour. Nancy took a deep breath and called her father.

"Dad," she said, "I need your help." She quickly explained why she was calling.

"That's great news!" Carson said excitedly. Nancy could also sense the relief in his voice. "Hold on, I'll get Levine's home phone number."

Nancy waited. In a minute her father came back on the line and gave her the number. As they were about to hang up, Carson warned her to be careful.

"You don't know that Allard isn't after you right now," he said.

"I know," Nancy told him. "That's why I want to call Levine right away."

"There's the doorbell, Nancy. I've got to go. Call me back as soon as you have some news."

"I will," Nancy said, hanging up.

As Chris, Kate, and Cheryl watched expectantly, Nancy dialed Levine's number. "Joe Levine, please," she said. There was a pause, and Nancy mouthed "He's coming" to Chris and Kate.

"Mr. Levine, it's Nancy Drew." Nancy was about to tell him about the safe deposit box and her suspicions, but the district attorney cut her off.

"What's he saying?" Kate asked. Chris signaled for her to be quiet.

"Yes, I understand," Nancy said. "Can I call you back? I'm here with Chris and Kate now and I should tell them. I'll call you back."

Nancy hung up the phone and turned to the Gleasons and Cheryl. "I've got some news you ought to hear," she said carefully. "The police did a handwriting analysis on your father's note. Although it's a close imitation of his handwriting, it doesn't match."

"What are you saying?" Chris asked, holding his breath.

"Joe Levine's come to the same conclusion you did. That someone killed your father."

Kate reached out and fell into her brother's arms. "We were right all along," she said, crying into his shoulder.

"For what it's worth," Chris said sadly. "Does he have any idea who would have done it?" he asked Nancy.

"I didn't get a chance to ask. But I'd be willing to bet that Dennis Allard is behind it."

Nancy led Cheryl over to the sofa and sat her down. Chris and Kate stood in the kitchen, holding on to each other and talking softly. She decided to leave them alone for a little while to let the news sink in.

Finally, after five or ten minutes, Nancy went over to them. "I know this isn't the best time, but we have to plan our next move. I have to call Levine back and I want to be able to tell him that you can go with him tomorrow to the bank to get into the safe deposit box."

"I can handle it," Chris said. "I'm just glad that this whole thing is coming to an end."

"Good," Nancy said, picking up the phone. Within a few minutes she had arranged for Chris to go along with the DA to the bank the next day to recover the evidence.

Nancy was just hanging up the phone when the door to Gleason's apartment flew open. She put the phone down. Chris and Kate froze.

Cheryl put her hand to her mouth, suppressing a scream.

Standing in the doorway were Dennis Allard and Peter Nicodemus. They both had guns. And between them, with his hands tied in front of him, was Carson Drew.

Chapter

Sixteen

"Don't you even want to say hello to your father, Nancy?" Allard asked. "You two might want to enjoy what little time you have left."

In disbelief, Nancy let out a gasp. They had been so close! She could tell her father was struggling to remain calm, but he was breathing heavily, and his face was ashen.

"You—" Chris shouted, throwing himself at Dennis Allard.

"Chris, stop," Cheryl cried. But it was too late. Allard had evidently expected the charge, because he was ready.

Chris had come at Allard headfirst. Allard

stepped to the side and brought the butt of his gun down on Chris's head as he sailed past him. Chris slumped to the floor, unconscious.

Cheryl let out another cry and ran over to where Chris lay. Kate put her hands to her mouth in horror.

"That should show you we're serious," Nicodemus said to no one in particular.

"I didn't doubt it," Nancy answered. She exchanged a look with her father. "Be ready," it said. He nodded almost imperceptibly.

Chris was coming around, and Allard poked at him with his foot. "Get up, hot shot," he said. "You're an important part of our plan, and we can't use you if you're unconscious."

Nancy tried to keep her thoughts straight. What did Allard mean? Why would Chris Gleason be an important part of his plan? What did the two men have in mind?

Allard pulled Chris to his feet. Nicodemus handed his gun to Allard and used clothesline to tie first Cheryl's and then Kate's hands together. Nancy noticed with relief that he was tying them together in front rather than behind their backs. Mobility would be crucial if they were to manage an escape.

"Be careful," Allard said. "We don't want there to be any marks."

"I remember," Nicodemus said sullenly. All the charm Nancy had observed in both Allard and Nicodemus had disappeared.

Nicodemus came over to Nancy, holding out the clothesline. "You're next, girl detective," he said with a sneer.

Nancy held out her hands and kept her eyes not on Allard or Nicodemus, but on Cheryl and Kate. She was trying to judge how much help they could be. Not much, she decided, when she saw that both girls were blinking back tears.

Nicodemus had finished tying Nancy's hands together. The rope was fastened too tight for Nancy to get any slack.

"Ready?" Allard asked. Nicodemus nodded and then picked up a brown shopping bag he had left just inside the room. He dropped the clothesline into the bag.

"Follow me," Allard said, and he gave Nicodemus his gun back. Allard drew another, smaller gun from his inside jacket pocket. He held the larger revolver in his right hand, and the smaller gun in his left. Then he motioned for Chris, Kate, and Cheryl to go ahead of him out the door.

Nicodemus put his gun into Nancy's back and pulled Carson along after him.

"Don't try anything, Drew," he said. "You wouldn't want to be responsible for another death, would you?" He gave a sadistic, nasal chuckle.

As Nancy felt the gun's barrel in her back, she tried to think of a plan. There had to be some way out of this, she thought. Maybe someone would hear them and call the police. Maybe they could disarm the men. But that was hopeless with their hands tied, she realized.

Nicodemus pushed Nancy after Allard down the long hallway to the elevator. Her father was at her side.

"What do you think they're going to do?" Carson mouthed.

"I wish I knew," Nancy mouthed back.

Allard was at the elevator, holding the door open. He herded the Gleasons, Cheryl, and Nancy and her father inside, then let the door close after he and Nicodemus had stepped in.

He pushed the button for the basement, and the elevator descended with a slow and steady creaking noise.

Nancy thought about making a move, but they were trapped inside the elevator. Even if she could disarm Nicodemus, Allard would turn a gun on her immediately.

She couldn't try anything heroic unless the others were prepared. Nancy nudged her father, who nodded his head. Then she tried to make eye contact with Chris, but his head hung down to his chest. He was barely conscious.

Before Nancy could think of anything, the elevator stopped at the basement. Allard put both guns in one hand, pulled the door open, and waited while Nicodemus shoved Nancy and her father out of the elevator.

Allard followed, both guns held on Chris, Cheryl, and Kate. Nicodemus had stopped, and Allard was shouting directions at him across the small hallway.

"Down there, around the corner. The room with all the junk in it." He had obviously been there before, Nancy thought.

"Hurry up," Allard said. "We're running out of time."

Nancy darted a look to her left before Nicodemus pushed her down the hall. There it was, the small door that led to the alley behind the building. Dim light showed through its dirty window.

Nicodemus pulled her down the short corridor and around the corner to the right. They were in a dirty room piled high with old furniture, mattresses, and cardboard boxes full of newspaper.

"Perfect," Allard said, coming around the corner. He turned on an old electrician's light hanging from a rusty metal pipe that ran along the low ceiling.

Allard sat Cheryl and Kate down on some boxes. Nicodemus kept his gun on Nancy and her father as he reached down into the bag. He pulled out a red-and-yellow metal can, clearly marked Gasoline.

With a shock, Nancy realized there had to be

only one reason for that can. Allard and Nicodemus were going to set the building on fire and let them all go up in flames with it!

Chris saw the can. "You're not thinking about—" He couldn't finish the sentence.

"Not right away," Allard said. "That's step two. First, we need to worry about step one."

"You're not going to get away with this," Nancy said. She tried to sound as threatening as possible. "The district attorney is on his way right now. He knows we're here."

"My plan takes all that into account," Allard said with a sneer. "As soon as I caught you in my building this afternoon, I realized it was only a matter of time before the DA was involved."

Nicodemus smiled and spoke. "And when I came to after you knocked me out, the first person I called was Dennis. He was the one who thought of this brilliant plan. Luckily, your father was home. Naturally, we convinced him to tell us where you were."

"But Nicodemus has been here before, right? The night he pushed Robert Gleason out his window," Nancy said.

Chris and Kate stared at Nancy. Carson drew in a sharp breath.

Allard laughed. "You're not a very good detective. Actually, if you really want to know, *I* was the one who killed Gleason." He stared hard at Nancy.

"Because you knew he had the proof you thought had been destroyed," Nancy added.

"Exactly." Allard's eyes narrowed. "I was sure every sign pointing to my guilt was gone. I even checked the computer records. But Cheryl here was better at finding something buried deep in the computer than I was."

Cheryl blinked back tears.

"What about the money?" Chris asked.

"They had it all along," Nancy concluded. "That's what you and Nicodemus used to start up the Convex Corporation, wasn't it? In fact, you were both in on the embezzling right from the start, weren't you?"

She shot a glance at her father. Somehow they had to keep them talking until they came up with a plan. Carson nodded imperceptibly.

"I can't believe you two," Carson said, his face reddening in anger. "Together, you let an innocent man go to jail. And then you were going to let me take the fall for it!"

Allard met Carson's eyes for the first time. "I didn't feel happy about it, believe me. But when Gleason started coming around again, I knew it was either you or me."

Nancy narrowed her eyes. "It wasn't just my father, either," she said. "You nearly killed Chris with that stunt you pulled at his garage."

"We thought maybe that trick and our little car chase would scare you enough to give up your investigation," Nicodemus confirmed.

"But you underestimated Nancy," Cheryl told him hotly.

"Mr. Drew, I have to congratulate you on having such a smart—and persistent—daughter," Allard said.

"Smarter than you think—" Carson began.

Nicodemus interrupted him. "We're wasting time, Dennis," he said impatiently. He pulled Cheryl to her feet.

Allard reached over and grabbed Kate. Then he gave Chris the smaller gun.

"You see the situation," he said to Chris, pointing out Carson and Nancy. "It's a shame, but you have no choice. If you want to keep your sister and girlfriend alive, you're going to have to kill Carson Drew and his famous daughter, Nancy."

Chapter

Seventeen

Nancy watched as Chris tried to push the gun aside. It was futile. With his hands tied together he was only able to knock it to the floor.

"You're crazy," he said, staring at Allard. "What makes you think I'd kill them?"

"Do you really want to risk it?" Allard leaned down to pick up the gun, keeping the revolver poised on Kate. He handed the gun to Chris again.

"Chris, don't," Nancy said desperately. She had to stop him from doing anything rash. "Can't you see what they're planning?" She pointed to the can of gasoline. "They're not going to let any of us go!"

"Listen to Nancy, Chris," Carson pleaded. "Now that he's told us he killed your father, Allard's not going to let you go. You know too much."

Cheryl looked as though she were about to faint. Kate stared at her brother.

Chris looked over at the can of gasoline and then back at Nancy and Carson. Nancy took a deep breath and tried, despite her fear, to plan some kind of escape.

Her mind was on the door to the alley. There was a slim chance they could all make a run for it if she could get them all moving at the same time.

Suddenly her attention was diverted by Chris leaping at Nicodemus.

The move took Nicodemus by surprise. He let go of Cheryl. She swung both her hands at his gun, sending it flying across the floor. Nicodemus stood there, disarmed and helpless, facing Chris, who was still armed.

Allard was so stunned he almost dropped his guard on Kate. She was about to squirm free when Allard strengthened his grip on her.

"Let her go, or I'll shoot him," Chris shouted.

Nancy stared at the gun that had flown out of Nicodemus's hand. She couldn't do anything until she was sure that Allard wasn't going to shoot Chris.

What happened next shocked everyone.

"Go ahead and shoot him," Allard said.

Nicodemus stared at his business partner. "Dennis, what are you saying?"

Nancy saw her chance. While Allard was concentrating on Nicodemus, she nudged her father, then ran for Nicodemus's gun on the floor. Before Allard had a chance to react, Carson Drew was on him, pounding away with his two fists at the hand that held the gun.

A shot went off as the gun flew from Allard's hand. Nancy dashed across the room and in one swift move kicked Nicodemus's gun farther across the floor.

Then Nancy saw that her father was still wrestling with Allard. She hurled herself at the two men.

"Let go of him," she shouted.

Allard let go of Carson and looked up at Nancy. He tried to pull himself off the ground, scrambling to run away.

Nancy sent a swift karate kick into Allard's chin as he tried to get up. He groaned and rolled over. Dennis Allard was trapped at last.

Still shaking, Nancy knelt down and spoke softly to her father. "You're okay, aren't you?" she asked.

Carson sat up and managed a weak smile. "I'm fine, Nancy. A little bruised, but fine."

Cheryl came over to Nancy and Carson, a dull kitchen knife in her hands. "I found it in one of the boxes," she explained, working at the clothesline tying Nancy's hands together.

With a few moves, Nancy's hands were free. She cut Cheryl's bonds, then Cheryl went to work on Carson's and soon had them untied as well.

Chris Gleason approached Nancy, holding out the spare clothesline. Nancy looked over at Nicodemus and saw that Chris had already tied the man's hands behind his back.

"Do you want the honors?" he asked, pointing to Allard.

"I think you can probably manage," she said, taking a deep breath. She watched as Chris wrapped the rope around Allard's wrists and made several strong knots.

"Now let's get out of here," she said when Chris was finished. Then she turned to give her father a hug.

"I was worried there for a little while," Carson said, holding her in his arms.

"Me, too, Dad. Me, too," Nancy said, smiling up at him.

A few hours later they were all sitting in the Drews' living room. Bess and George were there, too, along with Hannah.

"So Allard and Nicodemus were in it together all along?" George asked.

"It looks that way," Carson said, putting his arm around Nancy's shoulder. "The two of them thought they'd gotten away with it, too, until Robert Gleason came looking for that evidence."

"But that's just incredible," Bess said, nibbling on a pretzel. "He was just going to sit back and let your career be ruined!"

Nancy stretched. It had been a long day. "I don't think Dennis Allard really cared about that. The only thing that mattered was that no one ever came after him again. Nothing was going to stop him."

"Now he'll be out of our lives," Chris said. He was sitting on the couch with his arm around Cheryl. "And we know finally that my father wasn't a criminal."

"Nancy—" Kate began.

"You don't have to say it." Nancy smiled. "I understand why you acted the way you did. It's okay."

"But I just have to thank you for believing in us, despite the trouble we caused you," Kate insisted.

Carson smiled for the first time since they had been back home.

"There's something you don't understand," he said. "Something I've only begun to appreciate." He went over to Nancy and put his arms around her.

"What's that, Dad?" she asked.

"That nothing can stop my daughter. Not when she happens to be River Heights's most persistent detective."

Nancy smiled. George laughed. Hannah chuckled. Bess giggled. Chris hugged Cheryl again. And soon everybody was laughing.

Nancy's next case:

Nancy and her friends are helping Ned with a college marketing project—introducing Spotless beauty cream to the public. Problem is, Bess and a lot of other people who tried the new product have been rushed to the hospital. Alarmed, Nancy decides to check out the company that makes Clearly, the rival cosmetic to Spotless. But the teen detective soon finds that someone has more to hide than blemishes in this case. A mysterious individual has laced samples of Spotless with deadly poison. Unless Nancy finds out who it is, she'll be the one who's rubbed out . . . in *SOMETHING TO HIDE*, Case #41 in the Nancy Drew Files™.